JENNA SLADE
THE ENEMY WITHIN

RICH BLECHER

TABLE OF CONTENT

ACKNOWLEDGMENT

I would like to thank all of our friends who have been instrumental in developing this book. They have been inspirational and supportive. I would like to thank a few people who were key in reviewing *Jenna Slade – Enemy Within* and providing constructive feedback in its development.

Thank you:

Jenna B.
Katherin G.
Vickey O.

Chapter 1

The scent of rancid cooking oil and rotting vegetables filled the air, the mix of vehicle exhaust made it more tolerable.

"What did I do to deserve this?" I called out to the graffitied stucco wall across from Yao Ming's restaurant, but only the roaches heard me as they scurried between trash cans.

After eight years with the FBI, I should have been investigating terrorist cells, or even money laundering, but here I was, cleaning up some animal parts left in a bucket that was called in as a hate crime.

I kicked an empty beer can across the alley. I had known it was going to be a crappy day the minute Senior Agent Kimmel brought up my arresting a senator's son—again. It was one time. I thought we'd gotten past that.

Now I was here doing penance in a filthy alleyway behind Yao Ming's restaurant on Calle Ocho, Miami's premier Cuban-American business district. Sure, at twenty-eight I was the youngest agent in our local bureau. My record was spotless. Well, at least virtually. But I deserved better.

Maybe I shouldn't have kept a picture of my father on my desk. The grumblings by colleagues over the years of potential nefarious practices by my father and his committing suicide didn't sit well with the Bureau, but I didn't care. He was my father. I was also confident that the last place he'd want me to work was in the FBI. He'd likely prefer me to work in some hospital feeding geriatric patients through a tube and sending their disarticulated, gangrenous toes off to some pathology lab. He wouldn't want me in a field where I would be in danger.

I lined myself up to field-goal kick the bucket full of animal parts down the alleyway, only to stop short knowing the mess it would create—a mess I would need to clean. Besides, I just got my favorite black wool suit and cream-colored blouse from the cleaners.

I ran my fingers through my shoulder-length brown hair and wanted to scream. This was the third time I'd been assigned to some ridiculous task masked as a crime. Ming likely had insulted a local competitor or copied a recipe from some immigrant-owned restaurant rival.

Just in case anyone was watching, I snapped a couple of pictures and concluded that I could safely classify this as a violation of statute 82.812. I would have to drop by the local Babalawo's residence and have a chat with him about members of his congregation dumping bloody animal parts throughout the city. Yes, Santeria was still very much alive in Miami.

Making sure not to touch any of the dark red mess, I cringed at the sight of the bobbing head and firmly placed the lid on the orange bucket, then lifted it to the edge of the dumpster. With one good heave, I pushed the heavy burden over the edge.

"There. Case closed."

I grabbed a trash bag from a can next to the dumpster and threw it over the bucket. I couldn't have Mr. Ming knowing what I'd done. I peered over the side of the dumpster, and the bloody mess made me cringe. I had hoped the lid would stay on—but then I realized it had.

Grabbing an old broom by the restaurant door, I used it to move a faded child's blanket to the side of the filth-coated dumpster wall.

A human hand jutted out from under a plastic trash bag—a hand with glossy pink fingernails.

Maybe this case wasn't as much of a waste of time as I thought it was. I pushed on the release lever to open the side of the dumpster, but it wouldn't budge. I grimaced and pulled myself over and inside, landing along the arm. There was no pulse. The smell of decay was more prevalent inside the dumpster, where the pungent smells outside of it were an excellent mask. She could have been in there for days.

Not wanting to disrupt the crime scene any further, I jumped back out of the dumpster and realized I'd need to change my clothes after all.

This isn't typically an FBI issue, but I knew that our office was investigating similar homicides.

A black Mercedes slowly drove by. A man in the back seat had his window down. He was fairly handsome with wavy hair and a five-o'clock shadow in the morning. He stared at me as I pulled out my phone and continued by. I followed protocol, called the local police, and then my senior agent in charge, Teresa Kimmel.

A thorough textbook search of the area turned up nothing, zero, zip, nada. Old, chipped-away stucco over concrete was standard in the area. I asked a few passersby how often they came by here, and if they'd seen anything unusual, but as I suspected, no one had.

I looked up at the all-glass office building across from Yao Ming's. Curious onlookers had gathered behind the many stories of glass, trying to get some excitement in their day as brightly flashing police cars arrived one after another. A man in a suit stood near the window on the top floor. I couldn't make out any details except for a dark suit, white shirt, and dark hair, but he faintly looked like the man who had driven by me not too long ago. My instincts were telling me that I should check out this company more thoroughly. A prominent sign on the building said Dark Enterprises.

Within fifteen minutes of the police's arrival, the entire alley was taped off and the forensics team was swarming with their white gloves and cameras. The local police were keeping security around the perimeter.

Ming and his staff were interviewed, as were every person in a two-block radius.

I stood with my arms crossed, watching the mayhem, wanting to be useful, but Special Agent Kimmel had taken over.

"Is this your first dead body?" she asked, handing me a cup of coffee. I'd known there was a café next door but didn't think to buy anything. Kimmel was a woman for all women to look up to. Making it to her rank in a man's world was inspirational for all female agents. She stood as calmly as if she were watching a construction crew work. Her curly salt-and-pepper hair and short stature just masked the rumored wolverine inside. Someone with many hard knocks in her career and the scars to prove it.

The gray, decomposed corpse once had been a lovely woman. Someone had thrown her away like trash. A meat thermometer stuck out of her liver, used by the medical examiner to determine how long she'd been dead.

"Other than the cadavers in training, I don't see too many dead bodies while teaching stranger danger to kids. Do we know who she is?" I cringed at taking a jab at her regarding some of my assignments, but I wanted her to know I was ready for more.

"Not yet. We'll let the team gather everything, and we can sort it out later. No missing persons report on this description."

I nodded as the medical examiner's team placed the young woman in a black bag and lifted her out of the dumpster, which was now surrounded by the rotting refuse that had been pulled out to minimize movement of the body. Including that messy bucket of animal pieces.

My impatience got the best of me. "I want this case." My intention to strike a more subtle tone hadn't quite reached my mouth.

"I figured you would. This typically would be given to the police, but Agent Wilson has two other, similar cases where young ladies were found in dumpsters in the past few years. I think it might be related, so he'll likely have this one too."

Agent Fender Wilson was a senior agent who had spent almost the same amount of time in the Bureau as Kimmel had. He mentored two other agents, Jimmy Baxter and Seth Porter. Baxter was probably the dumbest agent in the FBI. How he got through the academy was still a mystery. But Porter and me . . . well, we'd gotten a little closer over the past couple of years, but I cringed that his mentor, Wilson looked more like a used car salesman than an FBI agent with a slimy personality to match.

"Fuck Wilson!" I exclaimed, loud enough that everyone in earshot glanced at me. "Wilson's cases don't involve animal sacrifices, now do they?"

Kimmel laughed and shook her head. "No. . . no, they don't. But regardless, you're not going to work a homicide case solo yet."

I looked to Yao Ming, who studied me with an angry expression. An expression that said I had just ruined his day. Perhaps if he hadn't reported a hate crime due to someone leaving a bucket of lamb parts on his doorstep, he wouldn't be in this situation, but then again, I wouldn't have found the body.

We both took a sip of our coffee as the back doors of the white coroner's car closed.

"Where's our Jane Doe?"

Agent Wilson had appeared behind us, followed by Baxter and

Porter. He was wearing the same tweed jacket and black pants he wears every day. His pale face had signs of a lifetime of acne and smoking. He pushed his jelled hair back along his head as they approached.

"We've got it from here, Agent Slade," Baxter boasted as he approached the medical examiner's vehicle. The medical examiner was Dr. Becky Jefferies, approximately fifty years old, short and slender with dirty-blonde hair. Baxter appeared to be doing all the talking while she just nodded and then got inside the vehicle.

Rage built up inside me when Kimmel placed her hand on my shoulder. "Agent Wilson, I want Agent Slade to help you with this case."

My poker face slipped—a smile may have appeared at the corner of my mouth.

"With all due respect, ma'am, I have my team. This may be the same killer we're investigating."

"Well, then since you're no further along after two years, I think a woman's perspective may be a welcome addition. Don't you, Agent Wilson?"

I couldn't help but grin, not only because I'd gotten my first murder case, but because it was enjoyable to watch Wilson clench his teeth behind his smile.

"As you wish. I'll have her read into the case tomorrow morning."

"Very good. And Wilson . . ."

"Yes."

"I'll be checking in on progress more frequently."

Wilson nodded. If he could shoot daggers out of his eyes, I'd already be dead by a thousand cuts.

"I'll read you in first thing in the morning," he said.

"Thank you, Agent Wilson," I said calmly, but behind the professional demeanor was a victory party. "I look forward to working with you."

Kimmel's voice was low. "I want you to keep me posted on everything that's happening. Do not do it at the office. I'll set up meeting times and places to discuss what you've learned."

Confusion consumed me, but I didn't want Kimmel to see it on my face. Was I added to this case to be a spy? Then again, I didn't want to do anything to risk being taken off it. "Do you think . . ." I began cautiously.

"Let me do the thinking!" she snapped. "I want you to investigate. If you're half as good as your father was, you'll get to the bottom of what's happening." She looked me over, likely at the stains from my brief dumpster dive, then leaned in. "Please go home and change."

Chapter 2

I went home, took a shower, and did some research on Dark Enterprises while waiting to be read in by Wilson the next morning.

The official website showed a collage of ships, planes, and trucks superimposed over a globe. I clicked on the company's leadership and met Trevor Dark, CEO. Definitely a looker. His dark hair and well-groomed goatee paired handsomely with his suit and red tie. He might be in his early fifties, but I was confident he attracted women of all ages.

I clicked on the many links embedded within the website, which took me to pages documenting their world operations and volunteer work, like feeding needy villages and transporting much-needed supplies worldwide. It appeared to be a very philanthropic company. A company many would be proud to work for.

A text came in from Porter. *I wanted to take you right there in the alley. I want you more than once a month!*

I looked around to ensure no one was looking, then laughed to myself as I realized that I was alone in my house. It was silly. Sometimes he made me feel like I was in high school again and I needed to make sure my father wasn't around.

Bring your A-game with you, and maybe I'll consider it.

I will, Jenna. Just be ready.

I stepped outside to check the mail and froze—a body was face down in my front lawn.

I sprinted to what I was hoping wasn't another homicide as I quickly scanned the area for anyone who might appear suspicious. An arm moved, and I sighed in relief. It was my neighbor Kenny.

"Kenny! Are you all right?"

He rolled over and replied, "Hi, Jenna. You look much bigger from this angle."

Rolling my eyes, I reached down to grab his hand. "Come on, Kenny. Let's get you up. What happened?"

"I must have tripped on a crack in the sidewalk, or something . . . that I don't remember, and while lying in the grass, my memories came back of when I was in basic training and had to do a low crawl."

Realizing he was okay, and I helped him stand.

"Thanks." He spoke softly with the sly half smile and brushed some grass from his pants. "How are you today?"

Kenny was known as the kindest man in our neighborhood, and he was loved by many of our neighbors. He had lived in this community for over forty years. At least, that's what I'd heard from others. My father never talked about him, but I did see the two of them talking from time to time in the front yard during one of Kenny's walks.

"My daughter is coming to visit," he continued. "I haven't seen her in—"

"I'm sorry, Kenny," I interjected. "I need to get ready for a meeting. Maybe we can catch up another time?"

Kenny lingered on the edge of my lawn. "Okay. Maybe tomorrow?"

"Sounds good. I'll try," I responded hastily. "Have a good day, Kenny."

Guilt gnawed at me for being so short with such a kind man. The few times I'd talked with him, he was funny and told interesting stories. But I had a date with Porter tonight and wanted to get ready.

After a long bath and half a bottle of Chardonnay, I wrapped myself in my burgundy silk robe and slippers, and walked downstairs to my father's study. My father's heavy oak door always opened slowly and made a low, dull squeak.

His study was more of a temple now. The lingering scent of his cigars often brought me to tears before I even looked at the many pictures on the walls and tables. There was one of him in standard

FBI battle gear, holding an assault rifle while posing with colleagues; one of him in a helicopter, sporting a full set of assault gear; and several taken on fishing trips, where he and others caught giant marlins. Almost every photograph included his partner, Scelisi, who worked with him for decades. Scelisi had been like a brother to him, more so than his actual brother, Jake. Other than hanging an old picture of the two of them in their twenties, my father didn't like to speak of him, only saying that he'd gone to prison and died many years ago.

The best picture of all, however, was the one in the middle of his desk next to his computer monitor. He was hugging me when I graduated from high school as the valedictorian. The tears in his eyes made my hard work worthwhile.

It now had been nine years since he died, but I'd never gone through his desk. Why would I when the Bureau cleaned it out? His clothing still hung in his bedroom closet while I used my mother's. Something deep down inside me didn't want to admit he was gone.

I sipped my wine and pulled open the lower drawer of the desk. He had numerous file sleeves, but they were empty of actual files. I closed the drawer, swiveled in his luxurious leather chair, and looked around at his life.

He had enjoyed life too much to have taken it himself—I just knew it.

I wiped the tears from my cheeks and studied the picture of him with my mother and me as a toddler at some picnic. After she died fifteen years ago, he had his work to keep his mind focused—and sometimes, only his work. Sure, he'd attended key milestone events, but other than that, he seemed distant. It would often be days before he returned a call. When I'd jokingly ask where he went, he would just say skiing in the Alps. I had laughed every time, because he didn't ski. I was never sure why he wouldn't tell me, but I assumed it was on some investigation, or maybe training foreign officers who were equivalent to FBI agents.

The FBI had thoroughly cleansed his office after his reported suicide. I had my doubts, but that was the official report. Scelisi oversaw the sweep to ensure no one messed anything up. I'd been on a few of them, and although I always respected other people's belongings, some agents did not. Scelisi said they wanted to be sure to collect any confidential information he may have kept here for his cases.

Scelisi's monthly checkups on me typically involved asking how I was doing, and what cases I was on. In return, I asked him how I could get ahead, and what he'd been up to for the past month. It seemed that he never had fun, but I kept asking. He would mostly stare at my father's many pictures and then leave.

An almost childish euphoria filled me when I spotted the little pink clay piggy bank I'd made him in third grade. It actually had a good profile of a pig, although the small slot in the top was too small to fit a quarter through. Still, it was the perfect size to store dimes. Not knowing what to make, I'd seen a picture of Arnold the pig on the cover of *Charlotte's Web*, and preferred that over making a spider.

I shook the little swine and was saddened, yet not surprised, that there was no jingle. Then I frowned—the curly tail was broken. A sudden flash inside the slot made me stop spinning and lean closer to the light. There, a flash of something shiny through the hole. It was hardly noticeable unless the light was just right.

I shook it harder, but it didn't make a noise. Whatever was in there was tightly wedged inside.

It doesn't look like a coin. Hmm.

I shook the pig a little harder to dislodge it, but it didn't work. Removing a letter opener from the drawer, I tried to pry the object out, all the while cursing my eight-year-old decision not to include a way to take the money out of it.

Maybe if I make the hole just a little wider . . .

The whole pig shattered into my lap. There, among the pink-clay-pig pieces, was a strange key. There were no teeth, but it had small green bumps along the side where the teeth should be.

After holding it up to the desk lamp, I saw what almost looked like small circuit boards along one side of the smooth metal surface. A small letter G was stamped under what appeared to be a handle.

I thought about calling Scelisi, but something in the back of my mind said I should investigate more before getting anyone else involved. A key like this had to be important.

I looked at the clock on the desk . . . 7:59. Punctuality was one of Porter's qualities. Fortunately, I had enjoyed more of his qualities in the recent past and was looking forward to enjoying those qualities soon.

I took a picture of the key with my phone, then realized I

couldn't leave it out anywhere. After one last glance around the room, and taking in one more deep smell of his lingering cigar scent, I closed the door and headed to my bedroom to hide the newfound treasure in a secure spot I'd never needed to use—until now.

My heart raced when I heard a knock, right on time.

The moment Porter walked through the doorway, he pinned me against the wall and kicked the door shut behind him. A thrill coursed through my veins as his lips passionately pressed into mine.

I giggled in between breaths. "I knew you would arrive exactly at eight!"

He pulled the tie to my robe, slid it from my shoulders, and gazed up and down my body with a heavy inhale. His hands freely roamed my body, building up my fire within.

"Damn, you're so hot," he growled. The hunger in his voice only intensified my arousal.

I took his hand and whispered, "Let's go upstairs."

Exhausted was an understatement. Porter had not only brought his A-game, he'd brought his A-plus game tonight.

"Wow, that was amazing. I really needed that," I panted while running my hand through his thick chest hair.

"Me too."

"Maybe I can work you up for round two?"

Porter sighed. "I would, but I've got to get up early to meet Wilson and Baxter."

"What are you doing? Is it the homicide case from this morning?"

He thought for a moment. "I'm doing the finest ass in the entire FBI, and no, it's a different task." He pulled me over and slapped my ass, leaving a bit of a sting, then leaned in to kiss me. He rolled out of bed, and I watched him get dressed. "Same time next week?"

"Have you told Wilson and Baxter about us?" Ugh, how did that blurt out? I winced, not sure if I wanted to know the truth.

He paused for a moment as he buttoned up his shirt. "No, but I'm sure since I don't give you shit, they've figured something out." He finished tucking in his shirt. "Would it be terrible if I did confirm us?"

I looked down, trying to find the words. We were both adults, and what we did in our personal lives shouldn't matter, but for those two to know would make life even more of a pain than it was. "Maybe not, but they're already assholes, and I don't want to give them any more ammo."

"Okay, then I'll keep it a secret."

I thought back to the first time Porter and I had hooked up. It was after the Christmas party last year, when I was giving him shit about working for Wilson. We were perhaps five vodka tonics deep, and I hadn't slept with a man in well over a year. We began tossing innuendos at each other, which somehow worked its way to his gun fitting into my holster, and the next morning, we woke up next to each other in the Marriott across the street, with severe headaches. After some aspirin and breakfast, we decided that an occasional hook-up wouldn't hurt.

After he left, I went downstairs to lock the door, pick up my robe, and pour some more wine, but I couldn't get the red flag out of my mind from Porter's defensive response. Were they somehow trying to keep me out of the investigation?

Chapter 3

While I was excited to finally work a murder case, I was not excited enough to bring coffee for everyone. Still, I definitely had a skip in my step, perhaps thanks to last night's little romp.

Baxter sat at Wilson's desk, looking through a folder.

"Are these the case files for me to look through?" I asked.

Baxter smugly replied, "Yeah, I guess Kimmel thinks you can solve this. It's not as easy as you might think. You're in the big leagues now."

"Oh, my . . . the big leagues. Then it's a good thing I wore my big-girl panties this morning. Do you have yours on?"

My father had taught me that you had to play hardball with your peers, or else they'd walk all over you. Lately, I'd been making it easy for them to do the latter, especially after the arrest of a senator's son the other day.

"Ha-ha. You're only here because Kimmel forced it. Just look through the records and get spun up." Baxter threw the folder on the table with a huff and walked away.

Baxter had only squeaked through the academy because Wilson vouched for him and wanted him in Miami. Baxter was a perfect example of the old saying, "You either know someone, or you are someone."

"Baxter, let's go. We may have a lead on the Jane Doe Blonde murder case," Wilson said as soon as he left the elevator. He only looked at me for a second before returning his gaze to Baxter. "Come on, let's hustle."

One of these folders was labeled Jane Doe Blonde. "You seriously have your cases based on a woman's hair color?"

Wilson replied, "She's unknown. Is there another feature I should have used?"

Baxter laughed. "Yeah, you could have called her Jane Doe B-cup."

He finally got a laugh out of Wilson while I shook my head and opened the Jane Doe Blonde file. Inside was a photograph of a beautiful young woman's body with a faint red ligature mark similar to the one on the body found in the dumpster yesterday.

"Hey, this may be related to the murder yesterday. I'm coming with you."

"Lots of women get strangled in this country, Agent Slade," Wilson replied. "It doesn't make them all related."

"We'll see. I'll follow you. I have something to do afterward."

We headed to an address in Calle Ocho, about five blocks away from yesterday's murder site. When Wilson stopped in front of a small alley, I pulled up behind him and headed to the alley entrance, shooting the homeless person on the park bench a furtive glance. He was too far away to be interested in what I was doing here.

This was not a good part of town. The sidewalks were littered with glass, food wrappers, used syringes, and empty alcohol bottles. People walked in groups with their heads down like they didn't want to waste time getting caught up in someone else's shit. More than one woman looked a little worse for wear and seemed as if they could use a bed for the night. This was not where Miami's best-paid escorts worked.

"Your lead is here? Where was the murder?" I asked.

"That dumpster in the alley." Baxter pointed to a rusty, dented dumpster about a hundred feet away. I was surprised the dump truck could empty it without it falling apart. The fresh graffiti was undoubtedly the only thing holding it together.

I was incredulous. "You're telling me that a woman with identical strangle marks found in an identical dumpster just five blocks away from yesterday's homicide has nothing to do with that case?"

Wilson surveyed me with steely eyes and pursed lips. He didn't say a word and walked down the alley.

On the other side of the dumpster sat a thin, grizzled man clutching an old blanket that looked more like a rag. He was huddled on the back stoop of a Cuban restaurant that carried the smell of sewer and garbage. The rattling din of traffic drifted down from the street, where people went about their days without giving a thought to his suffering.

"Hi Billy. It's been a while. How's life treating you?" Wilson asked.

He nodded and looked around with a faint smile. "I'm in Shangri La. What more could I ask for?"

"We heard you have information on a murder that happened here a while ago," Wilson said.

Billy held out his shaky hand. "A man has to eat. And it was four years and thirteen days ago."

Wilson nodded toward Baxter, who took out his wallet and gave the stranger a twenty. I was in disbelief how some drugged-out homeless guy could remember details of a murder over four years ago.

The man, in turn, grabbed a roll of cash from his jacket pocket and added the new twenty to it.

"Seems like you could feed everyone on the street with that wad," I said.

"Who's the witch?" he snarled, squinting at me.

Wilson frowned at me before returning to the witness. "So, what do you know?"

"I know that at around 3:00 a.m., a large man in a nice suit stopped by that dumpster, opened his trunk, pulled out a naked woman, and threw her in."

"You don't have a watch. How do you know it was 3:00 a.m.?" I asked. "It was over four years ago."

"Tell your baby girl to shut her piehole, or I'm done talking."

Wilson burned his shut-the-fuck-up look into my eyes, and then asked, "How did you know what time it was? It was a long time ago."

"Because that club"—he pointed to the door across from the dumpster—"closes at 2:00 a.m., and they throw out their leftover food before they leave around three, which becomes my breakfast treasure."

Baxter asked, "Do you know how big the man was, and what color suit he was wearing?"

"He was . . ." The man looked around, and then zeroed in on Agent Wilson. "Larger than you, but with your brown hair."

Baxter and I looked to Wilson.

"Well, obviously, it wasn't me," he said, then turned back to Billy. "Do you remember what kind of car, or anything else that stuck out?"

"It was an expensive black car that rich people drive. One with some chrome triangle in a circle, or something. Oh wait, I remember when a car passed, I saw another man in the driver's seat who had one dark eye."

"Like an eye patch?" I asked.

He sluggishly nodded. "Maybe it was an eye patch. I initially thought he might have been part-demon, but maybe that was the happy juice I took."

"By juice, you mean heroin?" I asked.

He lunged for me, but Wilson and Baxter stopped him.

"Shut the bitch up, or I'll cut her!" he said.

Wilson yelled, "Get out of here and go to the car!"

I clenched my teeth and walked back to wait.

"What the fuck was that?" Wilson demanded when they emerged from the alley.

"If he was on heroin, how can anything he said be trusted?"

"Even if someone is completely wired, at least part of what they see might be real. In his prime, that man had three PhDs with an eidetic memory. Use the informants, don't piss them off! And never judge someone by their appearance!"

My face burned with embarrassment. I clenched my fists in anger, pissed that it was Wilson who gave me this lesson on humanity. "I was just—"

"I will let you know when you can speak. I'm the lead agent on this case, and you're here to observe. Got it?"

I nodded as they walked to his Dodge Charger. At the door, he looked back at me and said, "Go cool off somewhere and get your head straight. I need a professional on this job, not some loose cannon trying to prove herself."

"What about Dark Enterprises?" I called out.

He paused for a moment and turned around. "What about them?"

"They were right across the street from the crime scene, and the entire wall is glass. Perhaps someone saw something."

"Stay away from them!" Agent Wilson spat. "They have nothing to do with this case."

"But—"

"That's an order, Slade!"

He ducked into his car and slammed the door shut. The tires squealed as he drove away. Showing off his testosterone, no doubt.

"Fuck you, Wilson!" I yelled, then looked around to see if anyone was in earshot. There was a man on the bench a hundred feet away, but he didn't stir.

Since Wilson practically said to go away for a while, I drove to Miami's oldest key maker and locksmith, whose last name happened to be Locke. When the old pocket watch my father had inherited from his grandfather wasn't working, I'd brought it to the repair shop next door as a Christmas present. I had stared in that lock store for what seemed like an eternity, amazed at so many old locks.

The clock shop was sadly gone, but Locke's Locks seemed unchanged. Inside was a glass case filled with dozens of locks. Each was different in shape and material, some old enough to belong in a museum. They ranged from gold-colored ancient Greek locks to ones made from titanium. I did a little research on the key, but other than finding out it was a digital key, there wasn't much information on the Internet describing it.

"Greetings, miss. Is there something I can do for you?" An elderly man with a hunched back and thick glasses stepped out from behind the curtain. His wild gray hair stuck out in every direction, and his eyebrows followed suit, yet he had a smile that could thaw the coldest of hearts.

"I'm Agent Slade." I displayed my badge. "I'm trying to get some insight into a key I've never seen before." I showed him a picture on my phone.

"May I?" he asked. I handed it to him and watched him zoom in on the picture. "Very rare key indeed. Used for expensive safe-deposit boxes, mostly with private banks."

"What's a private bank?"

"This type of banking is usually a non-connected institution where the affluent can store their assets without fear of being tracked or identified."

My dad was an FBI agent. Why would he have the need for such a bank? "Where would I find one?"

"It's hard to say. Some islands in the Caribbean might use such a key. Switzerland, perhaps the Seychelles."

"Is there one here in Miami?" I asked.

"I'm not aware of any, but that doesn't mean a company wouldn't have one. Usually, a key like this has biometrics saved in its chips."

"Its chips?"

He zoomed in on the tiny bumps where the teeth would be. "These are tiny microchips that store the biometrics of someone— or, perhaps, multiple people. You put the key in a small slot, and then, depending on whichever biometric device was connected, you apply that verification, and it opens the lock."

"How would someone open a box or safe with this key that doesn't have the biometrics?" Short of digging my father from his grave, there was little way I could match his exact DNA.

"It may be nearly impossible. Such secure places are created to offer the ultimate security."

"Thanks, Mr. Locke. I appreciate your time."

"You're welcome, Agent Slade. Have an excellent day, and good luck in your search."

Chapter 4

The office was nearly deserted when I returned. A couple of agents were talking about an upcoming drug bust, and a light shone from Kimmel's office, but she wasn't present.

The folders from this morning were still on Wilson's desk. After a deep breath, and feeling the need to redeem myself after this morning, I sat down and reviewed them, starting with Jane Doe Blonde from four years ago.

At the academy, I'd studied many cases with grotesque photos. Murder. Rape. Dead bodies that were once someone's son or daughter, mother or father. But now I was investigating a body discarded like trash.

Something soft—a wide rope or strap, and likely from behind—was obviously the murder weapon based on the severity of the trauma at the front of her throat. She was of European descent and seemed to have been quite beautiful when she was alive.

I went through the toxicology report, which showed a blood

alcohol level of .20. It was high enough to where she couldn't drive, but not high enough to pass out. There were multiple contusions on her pelvis, likely from violent intercourse, and patterned bruising around her wrists, presumably from a pair of large hands, given that there were no signs of ligature tie marks.

Her profile listed no background information. No fingerprints, no mailing address, no evidence of her existing. "In this era, how could that be?" I mumbled.

"How could what be?" Kimmel asked from behind me.

"Oh, Agent Kimmel. I was reviewing the murder cases Wilson gave me, and this first victim has no history. Not even fingerprints."

"That is puzzling, isn't it? Perhaps she didn't exist?" Kimmel suggested in tone bordering on sarcasm.

Was she playing with me or wanting me to develop my own theory?

"I don't see a DNA history here," I said. "Perhaps that could tell us something?"

"Good questions," Kimmel said as an encouraging smile flashed across her face. Then she disappeared into her office.

I stared at her door, wondering what the hell she was doing. She obviously wanted me to think outside the box, but she wasn't helping me. Or was she?

I opened the folder titled Jane Doe Brunette. *These guys are such assholes.*

The woman in the medical examiner's photographs was Middle

Eastern, approximately thirty years of age, killed two years ago. The toxicology report showed a blood alcohol content at .15. She had been pretty tipsy when she died.

The cause of death was asphyxia caused by strangulation. It also showed bruising on her wrists and pelvis. Hurriedly double-checking the previous folder, I realized that a postmortem rape kit hadn't been conducted on either victim.

And what was even more astonishing—Jane Doe Brunette had no history, prints, or DNA profiling on file either.

How the hell could there be so much sloppiness in this investigation?

I reached for Jane Doe Redhead.

"Hey, Slade! Solve those cases yet?" Baxter called out as he, Porter, and Wilson came off the elevator.

I swiveled around on my chair to face them. "Studying the overly informative case details right now, actually." I was hoping my sarcasm would cause some reaction—nothing. "Seems to be a lot of holes in this investigation." I set the unopened folder on the desk. "How much do you want to bet that the Jane Doe from yesterday has all the same details found in these folders? Same marks on the neck, same cause of death. Do you even have a folder started on her yet?"

Wilson eyed me, his expression stern. In another life, I might have thought his stocky figure and brown eyes were attractive, but everything about him, even down to his superiority complex, felt creepy.

"There we go, Wilson, Agent Slade has everything solved," Baxter cackled. He'd slicked his hair back just like his mentor, but still looked like a hobbit with a snaggle tooth. I understood our dental plan sucked, but come on.

Porter logged into his computer without saying a word. I wasn't about to have him defend me, but jeez, his coldness was surprisingly disappointing. I took a deep breath. It was what it was.

Wilson opened his desk drawer, pulled out a case folder, and tossed it before me. The name read Jane Doe Blonde #2. "There. The folder is started. Just waiting on the medical examiner's report."

Baxter laughed and slapped Wilson on the back. "The look on her face was priceless."

"Baxter, have you looked into the Bureau's dental plan?" I asked.

He swiftly snapped his mouth shut.

"Slade!" Kimmel bellowed.

"What did you find out from reading those files?" she asked as soon as I closed the door behind me.

I had only read two, but at the very least, several textbook forensics results were missing. I wasn't sure whether she was evaluating my ability to study a file or Wilson's incompetent investigative work.

"There are a lot of missing pieces. But I'm sure we'll get there."

I knew I should trust my boss, but why wasn't she familiar with the lack of information in those folders? After four years, why now?

Why was I really on this case? The missing pieces seemed way too obvious. Still, something told me to hold off. Perhaps Scelisi could help figure out the politics. He'd always said I could call on him whenever I needed to.

"Sounds good. Keep me posted on everything you find out. And Slade—tell me before you tell Wilson."

"I'd just like to thank you for putting me on this case."

"Jenna, I see a lot of potential in you, but your over-aggressiveness has been your biggest fault. Don't do stupid things that get you highlighted by our leadership."

Kimmel's face had a slight resemblance to Michelle Obama's, but her hair was shorter, curly, and salt-and-pepper. She may have been small, but she was among the strongest women I'd ever known.

"Ma'am, is this about that—"

"Do you know how many senior-level agents and deputy directors I've had to talk to about that this morning?"

"But if you saw what he was doing—"

"Yeah, I get it," she interrupted, leaning back in her chair with her eyes closed, almost as though meditating. "That girl will be right back with him."

She was right, but deep down, I didn't want to accept it.

I looked around her small office. Kimmel's achievements were nothing short of heroic, from saving the vice president from an assassination attempt fifteen years ago to rescuing a dozen school children held hostage by a psychotic teacher.

Kimmel opened her drawer, pulled out a large bottle of antacids, and chewed a handful while staring at a picture of her sixteen-year-old daughter, Lareiah, on the desk. Lareiah looked like a younger Kimmel with long curly hair. She had been a lacrosse star and a straight-A student in high school. A daughter to be proud of, with a beautiful smile that practically forced anyone to smile in return. Something I rarely saw on her mother's face.

A terrorist cell that Kimmel was investigating had held Lareiah hostage, and even though they'd threatened to kill her family, Kimmel did her job and rescued her daughter. She'd killed the terrorists, but months later, on her daughter's way home from school, loyalists had filled Lareiah's car with bullets. Those criminals were also killed. To this day, no bodies were ever found. Kimmel vowed she would take down every bad guy until her last breath.

She stood, placed her laptop in her briefcase, and gestured for me to walk out of the office. "I have an appointment to get to. Good day, Jenna."

At least she used my first name—she rarely did that outside of social settings. I'd finally gotten my chance to do more than simple investigative work. I had graduated at the top of my class at the FBI Academy, and I should do more to prove myself to Wilson and his ass-lickers. Well, at least one ass-licker. Porter wasn't quite in that category, since he'd promised not to be part of the harassment, given we were in a discreet relationship. I just wished he would get away from Wilson and find someone else to work under.

As Kimmel finished packing her briefcase, I suddenly spotted a folder on her countertop along the wall. Most closed-out cases made their way to a filing cabinet, but Kimmel liked to keep some at her fingertips, especially if they involved political figures. Written on the cover of the folder was "Dark Ent."

"Is that something to do with Dark Enterprises?" I asked.

"Yeah, some audit turned up red flags, and we were tasked to handle it. I don't have a forensics auditor here, so it'll have to wait until I can find one."

"Can I take a look?" I asked. "Dark Enterprises is across the street from the latest murder scene. Perhaps there's something in there."

Kimmel flung her hand, gesturing to take it. "Take a look, but don't lose the file. I suspect there's nothing but numbers and trust fund names that would give any normal person a headache."

I didn't want to say too much about my looking into Dark Enterprises. The last thing I needed was to pursue that lead and get ridiculed for searching a dead end.

I went out to my desk and fired up my computer. With all the firewalls and security software, getting to the login screen took forever, so I went to retrieve a cup of burned coffee. Fortunately, a few teaspoons of powdered creamer took some bitterness away.

Porter wouldn't look at me. Something seemed off. Usually, he was waiting to wink discreetly at me, or make some enticing expression, but it was almost like he was no longer interested in me. It wasn't like him.

I dialed Scelisi's cell phone number and, getting his voicemail, asked him to call me back.

I returned to the three amigos. "So, what's our next move?"

"Perhaps you can tell us?" Wilson leaned back in his chair and looked up at me arrogantly.

"For starters, why don't we run DNA to find out if we get a match on the Jane Does?"

"Great idea," Wilson said. "Go down to the medical examiner and get that done."

Baxter and Porter looked confused.

"Okay, I'll get right on it," I said and grabbed the folders.

The medical examiner's area in the basement was like good scotch. You got used to it with time and repetition, but you wouldn't actually like it.

The elevator opened, and as always, the sharp, metallic scent of alcohol and, well, death assaulted my senses. I learned at the academy that a by-product of a body's decomposition was called cadaverine, which, like the word itself, reeked of death. Once I'd smelled it during an actual autopsy, I didn't care what it was called. I just knew it would take a while to get used to—if ever.

I walked down the glossy-tiled hallway and found the medical examiner eating a sandwich at her desk in the open bay. Dr. Becky Jefferies stood up when she saw me enter the lab. Two bodies covered with white sheets lay on the stainless-steel tables.

When you thought of a medical examiner, images of someone in their sixties with gray hair and thick glasses probably came to mind. Dr. Jefferies was beautiful, with her long ponytail and slender body beneath her white doctor's coat. I smiled at the unnecessary stethoscope around her neck. She took off her readers and set them on the desk.

"Hello, hi. How can I help you? I'm Dr. Jefferies. I don't think you've been down here before, have you?"

"Hi, Dr. Jefferies. I'm Agent Jenna Slade. Besides my initial tour when I was assigned here, this is my first time. I'm working on a murder case from a couple of years ago. Perhaps you can help with some information?"

She stared at me briefly. "Jenna," she whispered. It was as though she recognized me, but I didn't recall meeting her in the past.

"I'm sorry, have we met before?" I asked.

"Sure. Sure. Let me make some room for you." She didn't answer my question but picked up some files from a chair beside her desk and looked around to find a place to set them. The side tables were full, and the examination tables held the two bodies, so she finally set the folders on the floor. "Have a seat."

I handed her the Jane Doe files. She opened the first one and paused for a moment before paging through it. "Well, now, there really isn't much here on this one, is there?"

She should know what needed to be in these files. "No, Doctor, and the other one is the same." I cautiously tried not to point a finger. "I was wondering if maybe something was omitted from the autopsies, or perhaps the results just didn't make it into the folders?"

"Let's look in the database and see what we can find."

She logged into her computer, which also took forever to spin up.

During the awkward silence, I noticed an indent in her ring finger but no ring. "Are you married?" I asked.

She saw I was looking at her finger and rubbed at the narrow mark with her thumb. "Divorced. Been too devoted to my job. I had a relationship with someone a long time ago, but sadly, he died."

"It must be challenging to have a personal life while working down here so much."

The FBI logo finally came up on her screen.

"Wow, I didn't think any computers were slower than ours upstairs," I tried to joke.

"Yeah, this one is tied to several federal databases, so I can research during the autopsies more easily." She searched for the case number in the folder, and it didn't bring up anything. "What's the autopsy number on that file again?"

"It's M-A-7-4-8-9-6-2."

She entered the number. Nothing again.

"Here, try this one." I opened the other folder and read out the file number. "M-A-7-4-3-7-9-1."

That number also came up with nothing. *No File Found.*

"That's very strange. Every autopsy is entered into our database and is never purged," Dr. Jefferies said as she leaned back, staring at the screen. "Sorry, it doesn't look like I can help you."

Why would she give up like that?

"Maybe we can try the date," I suggested and looked at the date on Jane Doe Blonde's record. Dr. Jeffries smiled at me and looked at the file, and several case numbers came up. She scanned through a few weeks prior and a few weeks after but found nothing related.

"It still doesn't look like I can help you, Agent Slade. It appears from the toxicology report that these women were drunk and, perhaps, stumbled into the wrong place at the wrong time?"

She closed the file on her computer. I pondered a moment, trying to understand what was happening.

The blonde woman from the dumpster yesterday lay on the table, just as ghost-gray as she was yesterday when I saw her get zipped into the black body bag. "Have you examined that one yet?" I asked, pointing.

"I'm waiting on her toxicology report, but no fingerprint records exist."

"That seems to be a trend with all these women. Were you able to run the DNA by any chance?"

She stood, picked up the stack of folders she had set on the floor, and stood at my chair. "I appreciate your help with my job, but I'll take it from here, Agent Slade," she snapped. "I have a lot of work to do."

I received the hint loud and clear. She wanted me gone. I may have hit a trigger point with my questioning.

Not wanting to let on that I saw her discomfort, I scanned the other examination table, where a young man with an olive complexion, dark hair, and a goatee rested.

"Okay. I'm sorry if I overstepped my position. I'm working on this with Agent Wilson, so let me know if you find anything."

"Oh, Agent Wilson?" Dr. Jefferies suddenly seemed annoyed. When she'd talked with him the other day at the murder scene, she hadn't looked happy either.

"He's upstairs and had me come down here."

She shook her head. "Is that right? He should be quite aware of the details associated with this case. I'll let you know if I find anything further."

That was strange. Did she and Wilson . . . ? Or did they have a falling out?

As I turned away, I glanced at the bodies again. "Just out of curiosity, why would these bodies come here instead of to the local authorities?"

"That, I don't know. I just do as I'm told." She turned away to grab her sandwich and continued to mumble, "Seems like the safest thing to do."

I had to talk this through with Scelisi.

Chapter 5

Scelisi called just as I was pulling up outside my house.

"Jenna! I was delighted to hear from you. How are you doing? Is everything all right?"

"Hi, Scelisi. I've finally been assigned to a homicide crime."

"That's great! Way past overdue, in my opinion."

"Thanks. I'm glad someone believes in me."

Talking to Scelisi was the closest thing I had to talking to my father. Although I hadn't always needed a shoulder, he'd been there. "I have some issues I wanted to discuss with you in person. Something regarding a case I'm working on."

"Sure, I'd be glad to. Are you free for coffee in the morning?"

I brought my car to a halt in the driveway, only to see that the front door was slightly ajar. Heart pounding, I reached for my service-issue Glock 9 from my shoulder holster and swiftly exited, surveying the quiet street for any signs of life—nothing.

"Scelisi, gotta go. I think someone broke into my house. I'll call you back."

"Jenna . . . wait!"

I hung up hastily before sprinting toward the door, adrenaline coursing through my veins as I steeled myself against what I might encounter on the other side.

My hand tightly gripping my gun, I nuzzled the door open. I tiptoed through each open room downstairs before hearing a faint squeak from my father's office at the end of the hallway.

Chills ran down my spine as I pressed myself against the wall and peeked inside. A man dressed in all black stood with his back to me. He held something in his hands. My finger drifted toward the trigger when he spun around, and we faced each other in utter shock.

"Freeze! FBI!" Though my stance didn't show it, I was trembling.

He remained frozen with some type of TSA-looking scanner. With a black ski mask and a bulletproof vest protruding under his black suit, it almost seemed like he was wearing a government-issued assault outfit.

"What are you doing here? What's in your hand?"

It almost looked like a—

My temples throbbed as I tried to lift my body from the ground.

"Easy does it, Jenna. Just stay there for now," Kimmel said.

Someone slid a soft pillow beneath my aching head.

"What happened?" I asked, touching the back of my skull, feeling the painful lump from the blow that had knocked me out.

"We were hoping you could tell us, but first, you need to get checked out at the hospital," a familiar voice said. "You had a nasty knock on your noggin."

"Scelisi?" I mumbled, trying to focus on him. Scelisi was about the same age as my father, but with short curly hair that was balding in the center, dressed in a standard black suit and white button-down.

"Will you please narrow yourself to one person?" It hurt to laugh, but everyone was blurry.

"I'm right here, Jenna," he said as I tried to clear my sight before feeling queasy again.

"Agent Scelisi called me straight away after you hung up with him," Kimmel said. "But we couldn't get here in time to catch the person who did this to you."

"They were searching my dad's office," I mentioned.

Kimmel asked, "Searching for what, exactly?"

"I don't know. I asked him what was in his hand, then I woke up in this spot."

"Jenna, did your father ever bring up a key at any point? A special key?" Scelisi asked.

I moaned to give me time to think. Why would he ask about the key now? After finding out what kind of key it was from the locksmith, I decided it was best to play dumb. "I can't remember, but the FBI took whatever they wanted after he passed away. You were here."

"Yes, Jenna . . . but this key is quite small and doesn't look like a regular one."

I held my head and continued to moan, unable to think straight.

The EMTs arrived. I would have rather passed out while they got me on the stretcher, so that I could avoid Scelisi's questions.

"We'll place a uniformed police officer in front of your house, Jenna," Kimmel said. "Are you sure you don't remember anything else about the incident?"

"Sorry, Agent Kimmel. I don't recall anything other than the intruder wearing a bulletproof vest, black stocking cap, and what looked like an FBI-issued assault wear."

She nodded at me, and then to the EMT, who carted me away.

"Did you have to put an IV in me?" I asked in the ambulance.

"Sorry, ma'am. It's standard procedure in the event you need further attention."

"I seem to be getting more attention than I need these days." I laughed and then my head throbbed in pain.

The doctor admitted me to the hospital overnight for observation, as he thought I might have a concussion. It took little convincing. Sure, I had seen three Scelisis, but the lack of any extra clothes or a toothbrush frustrated me.

The nurse gave me a sedative, but I couldn't sleep. Were those guys looking for the key I'd found in that little clay pig?

The plastic bin on a wall shelf held my clothes, identification, and gun. It had been risky to place the key inside my spare Glock magazine, but since I hadn't needed to use that magazine in eight years of working for the FBI, it was a reasonable risk to have thirteen fewer bullets.

"Jenna, how are you doing?" Kimmel asked as she appeared in my hospital room. She had one of the most stressful jobs I knew, but somehow had the kindest disposition . . . until you crossed her.

"The nurse just gave me a sedative and some painkillers, but I expect to get out of here tomorrow and figure out what happened."

"Jenna, what do you know about this key Agent Scelisi asked about?"

Shit.

"I don't know what he was referring to."

She nodded. "When you get out of here, take a day off to rest and find out if anything was stolen."

"Thank you, ma'am."

"If you remember anything else, let me know. I also think it's best to take you off the case while you recover." She walked to the door. "Good night, Jenna."

No, no, no. I can't be taken off the case! "I found a key hidden in my father's home office. I went to a lock specialist and learned that it's a key to some high-end vault, not typically around here—perhaps Europe."

"Thanks for letting me know. If the doc is okay with it, you can continue working with Wilson, but also continue reporting to me." She started to close the door, but then she opened it again. "Oh, and I'm going to call a friend for a favor. I want you to give them those photographs of the Jane Does. They'll do a facial recognition, and I'll share it with you when it comes in."

"Why don't you just send the photographs in?" I asked.

"Everything passed electronically is getting surveilled. I can't raise any alarms until I have more proof. It's one of the reasons why I decided to put you on this case."

"Proof of what?" I asked, trying to sort out where she was going. The sedative was suddenly working great.

"I'll fill you in when I can. It's best that you don't know some things." She reached into her jacket pocket and pulled out an old, cheap cell phone, the kind you prepay for. "Here's an untraceable phone. Only use it to call me, and I'll call you on it. There's one number already entered, under the contact name D. Call me when you leave the hospital, and I'll give you details on where to take those photographs of the Jane Does."

"What does D stand for?" I asked before she could leave.

She glanced in both directions, then back to me. "Deliverance," she said, and walked out.

Chapter 6

When I got home, Miami's finest was parked out front, just as Kimmel had promised. I waved at them and received a wave back. *Do they even know me, or would they let a stranger wave and walk in?*

The yard needed a little maintenance, but I'd decided it wasn't wise for them to work around the house right now. I could tolerate some tall grass for a few days.

The door was unlocked, but there didn't seem to be any damage. I tested my key to ensure it locked. Then I unlocked it and looked over the lock for any scratches but found none. *Whoever did this was good.*

My home security system was off-line. How was it off-line during the intrusion? I set the alarm every time I left the house. Someone knew how to disable that, too, as I'd never got a call about it being deactivated. Whenever the landscaper sent a rock through my window, I immediately received a notice on my phone. The motion sensor once had set off the alarm when I was out of town. The police showed up to find a mouse running across the kitchen floor.

I walked through the house, trying to notice if anything was out of place. The living room and kitchen looked good. In my bedroom, there were diamond earrings on my dresser. I shook my head, realizing how naive I was to leave expensive jewelry out in the open, but it assured me that this was no robbery. They were looking for something more specific . . . the key.

Perhaps one of my neighbors saw something? Kenny was the most likely.

The neighbors on either side had been home but saw nothing, and informed me they were adding a security system after what had happened to me. The neighbors across the street hadn't seen anything either.

"Jenna, was your house robbed yesterday?" Kenny was walking toward me, concern on his face.

"Yes, Kenny. Do you know something about it?"

"I've been sitting in that window every day since my beautiful bride of fifty years passed away. I was hoping to find anything to keep me . . ."

I had a feeling this would be a long story about his life on the block, but I let him continue. To my surprise, he focused quickly.

"The car was parked right there in front of that house . . ." He pointed to a house adjacent to the one behind mine. "A man sat in the car wearing a mask, and the other men walked between those fences. I didn't know where they were going until I saw the police walking around your house yesterday."

"Can you describe the car?" I asked.

"Oh yes, it was a Dodge Charger. I had a '66 Charger in my day. Wow, that was a nice car. I was popular with the ladies . . ."

"I'm sure it was an impressive car, Kenny."

"I met my wife with that car. One night, when we were at the drive-in—"

"I'm sure you had a wonderful marriage. Did you happen to get the license plates or remember the color?"

"It was a black Dodge Charger, but sadly, my sight doesn't reach far enough to see a license number. Still, I think the driver was talking on the phone before the others ran back from your house and got in."

"If you couldn't see the license plate, how did you know the driver was on the phone?"

"The man in the car had his elbow bent. If he wasn't on a phone, he was covering his ear, or something."

The tall fences would have made it easy to get to my house without anyone being the wiser, even during the day.

"Would you like to come inside for some coffee?" Kenny asked. "My home-care assistant brought over some delicious blueberry muffins."

His inviting smile was precious, but I needed to hunt down my intruder.

I put my hand on his arm. "Thank you so much, but I'll make sure to stop by soon. I have a busy day in front of me."

"Okay, another time then. I'll hold you to it!" He laughed.

I laughed also. "You do that. And when I visit, you can tell me all about your wife."

Back inside my house, I checked out my alarm system. After setting it, I went to open the door. The warning started, and I waited until the alarm went off. I instantly received a phone call from the security company.

"Hello, Ms. Slade. I wanted to advise you that your home alarm is going off. Would you like me to call the police?"

"I'm sorry, no, it was me. I forgot my code to shut it off for a moment." I entered the code, and the alarm shut off. "There, I got it now."

"Okay, Ms. Slade. Is there anything else we can do to assist?"

I thought for a moment. "Yes, my home was broken into yesterday afternoon. Do you show a record of any activity?"

"Oh, I'm so sorry. I don't see any activity on your account. Did you have the alarm armed?"

"I think I did. Do you keep a record of when I arm it and unarm it?"

"One moment, ma'am." A pause. "Ms. Slade, yes, we show you armed your alarm at 7:39 a.m. yesterday morning, and then it was unarmed yesterday at 3:47 p.m. I don't have any additional recorded activity until a few minutes ago."

"Can someone unarm my alarm without knowing my code?"

"We have one of the best security systems in the country, and I don't know of any incident of that happening. Typically, it would be a family member or a friend who might have your code."

"I live alone and have no family or friends with the code, but thank you."

She hesitated. "Ms. Slade, your alarm system runs through your home Wi-Fi system. If that doesn't have secure encryption, someone with technical experience might be able to access your alarm system through your Wi-Fi, but it would have to be a very sophisticated and experienced person."

I nodded, realizing I knew of a few organizations that would have that skill. "Thank you. You've been a great help."

My Wi-Fi had been set up by my father, and I just continued paying the Internet bill. *I'll need to get some experts here to check it out.*

"Hello, Ms. Slade? I'm Todd from Smart Tech. I'm here to check on your Wi-Fi," a young man in a black Smart Tech polo said when I opened the door. With youth and a dirty-blond manbun, he reminded me of some of the brilliant cyber security people I'd met.

"Thank you for coming so soon. Right this way," I said, leading him to my father's office.

"What seems to be the problem?"

"I want to know if anyone hacked my Wi-Fi or security system yesterday."

He stared at the Internet box with three blinking green lights. "Ma'am, I don't have information to determine that, but I can evaluate your password and give you more details about that?"

"Fine, yeah, go ahead." I was paying two hundred dollars for his immediate response, and all he would tell me was the password I already knew.

He plugged his laptop into my router, and an application appeared. I could type fast, but his speed was in an entirely different league.

Various colored graphs and charts flashed across the screen for a few seconds at a time as he ran through some diagnostics, but no screen stayed up long enough to read.

"Can you actually read that fast, or are you looking for something?" I asked.

"Each screen has a health function, and I just need to see one small metric. If it's good, I advance to the next screen. After doing this a few hundred times, it doesn't take long to scan through the pages. Here's your password. It appears it was set up in 2013. I recommend changing your password every six months to ensure better security. Some sophisticated equipment out there can crack any password given enough time. I also advise to use a sixteen-character password with a mix of numbers and characters. Would you like to change your password now?"

"Wait, 2013 . . . Do you have an exact date?"

"Yeah, sure, it was August 12. Is that a significant date?"

"It was two weeks after my father passed away, and I didn't reset it."

I stared down at the box, remembering the FBI rummaging through my house.

"Sooo, do you want your password changed?" Todd asked. "I highly recommend it."

"Yes, but if I do it on your laptop, then won't you have it?" I asked.

"Good question. Anything entered here goes directly to your router and won't be saved on my computer, but if you like, I can set up your laptop to do the same."

I thought for a moment. "Why don't you leave me the instructions to access this page? I'll set it up from my laptop later."

"Sure, I can do that."

"What are a few ways that someone could get my password?"

"Someone could park on the road and get into your Wi-Fi, and with the right hacking experience, they could get at anything connected to it. All it takes is someone connecting a laptop to your router and looking it up, as I did. Then they would have to run a decryption application to crack your password. Given what you had as a password, with the right processing power, they could have done it in perhaps an hour."

Other than Scelisi, I hardly had any visitors. No one other than Porter, but he always came over for a quick romp. He'd only spent the night twice, and even then, we didn't sleep much.

Todd unplugged his laptop from the router and did some additional typing. "I just sent you a PDF to the email you supplied, with the instructions on changing the password. I recommend you do it as soon as possible."

"Thank you, Todd. I appreciate your help."

Before he left, I asked. "Todd, how far away can someone access my router?"

He tilted his head as though he was reading some algorithms on the lenses of his glasses. "It would depend on the power of their transmitter and the aperture of their receiver. I would think someone sitting in a car . . . Perhaps not farther than a block away with advanced tech, but typically, it wouldn't be much farther than from the road in front of your house."

"Thanks, Todd. I appreciate your help."

Memories of at least a dozen FBI agents rummaging through our house those weeks after my father's death flashed through my mind. Each day, Scelisi was there to ensure I felt more comfortable with the disruption and that nothing got broken.

I vaguely remember that my Wi-Fi password had changed then too. But why?

All of this activity happened after I found that key, but how did they know I'd found it? Who were they?

Chapter 7

My pocket buzzed. It was D calling.

"Slade," I answered.

"Do you still have the case files with the photos?" Kimmel asked.

"Yes, I took a cab home, and they're in my car. Let me check."

Embarrassed was an understatement. I had been careless enough to leave confidential folders in an unlocked vehicle. Still, when you unexpectedly get taken to a hospital, it was hard to ensure everything was squared away first.

Thankfully, when I looked into the car, it was just as I left it: briefcase on the passenger seat. Inside the briefcase were the folders I needed.

"Yes, got it."

"Good. I'm sending an address where you'll meet a woman named Holly. She'll be expecting you. Just give her the photos and don't ask questions. She'll scan the images and give them right back. Got it?"

"Got it, but—"

Before I could finish my sentence, the call disconnected. A new text from D showed up with an address.

The drive to that address was a blur, not because of the blow to my head, but because my mind was doing gymnastics while thinking of the intruders' black Dodge Charger. Wilson had one, but why would Wilson want to get into my house? Did he know about the key too?

I shook off this thought and parked in front of a nice-looking house in a pleasant neighborhood. It was a typical two-story brick with wonderful landscaping. This was not what I had expected to find at all—no run-down trailer park home or warehouse.

When I knocked, a woman opened the door. "Hi, can I help you?"

"Holly?" I asked, and when she nodded, I extended the photographs.

She took them and closed the door. I half expected to be invited inside to wait, but I guess I was just going to have to hang out. I looked around the neighborhood, which was quite similar to mine.

After a few minutes passed, she reappeared and handed me back the items.

"Have a good day," she said before closing the door.

I glanced at the small fountain in the flower bed as I returned to my car. This felt like something straight out of a Tom Clancy novel.

When I returned to the office, the coffeepot was empty and Kimmel was gone.

My desk was just as empty as my leads, but I logged into my computer and searched for the murder victim I'd found in the dumpster. I tried to find her on Wilson's case list, but I didn't have access. I looked up Agent Baxter—nothing.

"What the hell does he even do?" I mumbled.

"What does who do?"

I rapidly turned. "Agent Kimmel. You startled me." She didn't even turn to look my way as she strode through the office in her cream-colored pinstriped suit, holding her briefcase.

"Did you accomplish the task I gave you?"

"Yes, ma'am."

"Good." She continued to her office.

I'd been hoping to prove myself with this homicide case, but now I was working on three unsolved homicides that all seem intertwined. A senior agent watched over the investigation, but he didn't have any records of the victims ever existing. A body had been recently discovered in a dumpster and taken for examination downstairs, but again, no record. And to top it all off, my house had been invaded by someone searching for a unique key my father had hidden in the piggy bank I'd made back in third grade.

With all these pieces flying around my head, I decided to go home and map out what I had so far on the large corkboard wall in my dad's study.

He had years' worth of photos pinned up there, most with Scelisi.

I collected all the pictures and placed them on an end table next to the leather sofa. Then I thought back to my academy days, where we learned how to set up a murder board. Even though I had gathered little evidence to connect anyone to anything yet, I wrote some names on sticky notes: Kimmel, Scelisi, Dad, the Key, Jane Doe Brunette, Jane Doe Blonde, Jane Doe Blonde #2, and Jane Doe Redhead. And then I included Wilson because I just wanted to.

I posted them on the corkboard and got some red yarn from my mother's old knitting set. I wanted to connect pieces of evidence, but after I placed the red yarn on a pin stuck into the board, I recalled the process from the academy and connected relationships but ended up with nothing more than a crushing headache.

My father's bourbon called my name. He kept that and his scotch in lead crystal decanters I'd gotten him for Christmas two years before he died. I poured a couple of fingers into the glass as the pieces of this puzzle spun around in my head. I looked down at the pictures I had set on the table and picked one up. My eyes narrowed. It was of my father, Scelisi, and Wilson—dated six months before his death.

Wilson had mentioned nothing about my dad, nor had my dad mentioned him, yet here they were together on a fishing trip. Even more reason to have him on the corkboard.

This just made the puzzle much more complicated. It would be easy just to say Wilson had killed the women, and close this case, but I needed more proof than him being an asshole.

I sat at the desk and opened the folder from Kimmel's office. It was a financial audit conducted on Dark Enterprises. If it weren't for Wilson ordering me to stay away from Dark, I'd be there today.

I'd had one training session on money laundering and wire-transfer fraud, but I wouldn't know where to start seriously investigating. Still, I scanned the file to see if anything popped out. But it was all numbers and names. Then I read the reports giving background information about Dark Enterprises. It was a company that made three billion dollars a year in revenue, and conducted worldwide logistics operations. They moved government supplies, building supplies, artwork, shipping containers, defense equipment, and even had special ships that transported boats with water inside.

From there, a long list of companies all over the world connected to millions of dollars in each account. Another list of trust funds filled a page, with various companies as their trustees. Each was in some offshore account in the Caribbean, South America, or Europe, and there were several layers of trust to hide the activity.

Many of the trust funds had a name. There were the Zahra Trust Fund, the Emily Trust Fund, the Sueann Trust Fund, and more. I counted twenty-one trust funds, but only Sueann and Emily actually had a positive balance. The others were zero but not closed out. Emily had 121 million dollars in her fund, and Sueann had over 100 million.

I didn't understand how trust funds worked, but there appeared to be a connection between them and the listed companies. Each of those companies were subsidiaries of another company in Belgium, and other companies throughout the world, but all had one common denominator: They were all subsidiaries of Dark Enterprises.

There wasn't enough bourbon in this glass for the headache I was about to get trying to decipher this folder.

Hastily paging through the documents, I wondered if these accounting documents were from before or after an audit, as I couldn't decipher anything. There were two thousand bolts and fifty thousand nuts sent to Syria, five thousand screws shipped to Afghanistan, and twelve-hundred machinery parts sent to Sudan, not to mention other building supplies listed at different locations.

I fired up my father's desktop computer and looked up Dark Enterprises again. There were far more references to it than expected. Who would want that name? The company had representation in every major country. And within each of those countries were other named subsidiaries. How could anyone keep up with all of this? I couldn't even arrange sticky notes on a corkboard.

A knock alarmed me. I closed the computer and stashed the file in the top desk drawer.

Scelisi was at the front door.

"Scelisi! Hi, what brings you here? Oh, and thanks for calling in for backup the other day. I should have known better than to go in alone."

"You're right. But I'm glad you're okay. I wanted to see how you're doing."

A black Dodge Charger was in the driveway, parked behind my piece of crap. He looked back at it as well.

"I hope I get to a point where I can get a nice car like that," I said, then recalled Kenny seeing the same type of car parked on the street behind my house. Nah, couldn't be.

He laughed. "Yeah, it's a nice perk. We don't get many, so we've gotta appreciate what's handed to us. May I come in?"

Scelisi was like an uncle to me. I'd known him nearly my entire life, and he was in it more after my mother had died. I opened the door. "Yes, by all means."

"Jenna, when we came by after your father's funeral, I thought we'd gotten everything, but we may have missed something. I believe he may have had a key. A unique and special key that may give access to important documents needed for a cold case."

The key again?

Part of me wanted to tell him because my father had trusted him. But asking for the key and having a black Dodge Charger? He was someone I had trusted for years, yet a deep part of me quickly decided not to trust him right now until I found out who had broken in.

"You're more than welcome to check through his office again, but I haven't seen any unique key."

His pursed lips told me he knew I was lying, but he nodded.

"You know, Jenna, there are some dangerous people out there who would stop at nothing to get it back."

"What kind of cold case do you suspect this key is connected to?" I asked.

"It may unlock some important information on a case your father was working on."

I stared at him to get a read and hide my developing fear. "I'll keep an eye out for it and let you know if I find it."

"Don't trust anyone in your bureau office, Jenna. I know you have to work with the other agents, but report anything suspicious to me. I'm here to help."

"I'll do that. But hey, do you know anything about a company called Dark Enterprises?"

He stared at me. "They're a terrible company involved in a lot of dark money and laundering, globally. Stay away from them."

"I'm not involved with them. I just ran across their name on a file."

"Don't get involved in anything to do with that company. I wouldn't want to lose you too. Remember, Jenna, call me with anything. I want to help you. Help you better than I was able to help your father."

"How could you have stopped him from killing himself?"

Scelisi had a somber expression. My gut told me he knew more. "I'll be going now. Be careful, Jenna, and call me if you need anything."

I watched him through the window as he drove out of the driveway, phone up to his ear. I swiftly pulled out my phone and snapped a picture before he drove off. Time to check on a neighbor.

Kenny's house had grown decidedly ramshackle these last few years. The missing pieces of siding, the broken railing on one side of the steps, and the moisture inside a window showed a significant lack of maintenance. Being alone and watching the day go by from your window would do that to a house.

"Jenna! You made it! Come on in. Can I get you some coffee?"

I realized I'd been brushing him off recently, so I decided to sit for a while. "Yes, I'd like that. I drink it black."

He mulled around in the kitchen as I walked into the living room. The many pictures of his wife and daughter filled the walls, showcasing their many years of marriage.

He set a cup and saucer in front of me with a small dish of what appeared to be a cobbler.

"Kenny, can you look at this picture and see if it's the same car you saw on the street the other day?"

I showed him the picture.

He squinted. "It looks like the same car, and maybe the same person, but I didn't see any details. I'm sorry. But come on and try the best apple cobbler you've ever had. My daughter memorized my wife's recipe and brings some when she visits now and then . . . usually more then than now. But she came to visit this morning."

My heart sank. "I'd be glad to," I replied. I took a mouthful of cobbler and washed it down with coffee. It was delicious.

He nodded. "It's the best, isn't it?"

"It's very good, Kenny. Thank you."

We talked about his daughter and how she lives in the Keys with her husband.

"Maybe I can introduce you to my grandson," said Kenny. "He's about the same age as you."

I smiled at how adorable he was, took another bite of cobbler, and sipped more coffee. "I'm sorry, but I need to get going, Kenny. I'll stop by again soon."

"Okay. Thanks for coming by, Jenna. I hope you find the guy."

I returned to my house, printed a picture of Scelisi in his car, and posted it on my corkboard. Then I opened the Dark Enterprises file again. Zahra was a unique name for a trust, and it was curious that the other names were all women's first names as well.

I looked up the name Zahra on my phone—a popular Middle Eastern name. Jane Doe Brunette had a Middle Eastern look about her. If the facial recognition identified that woman as a Zahra, then this case may have a lead with Dark Enterprises right in the middle.

I needed a data analyst, and I knew who just to call.

Chapter 8

scanned the folder again and found references to various animal names linked to accounts in Ireland, the Seychelles and Switzerland. This was a spaghetti bowl of exchanges that I couldn't understand even if I had a hundred years to do so.

I brought in the one person who might be able to help. Hamilton was an old classmate from the FBI Academy who had studied finance at Harvard and was now a forensics analyst. He was in Germany—not ideal for catching up—but he did owe me a favor.

Rather than calling him from my personal phone, I used the burn phone. This would protect us if anyone was tracking my calls. Kimmel said to only call her with it, but I could make this exception.

"Agent Hamilton."

"Hamilton. It's Slade. From the academy."

"Oh my God . . . Slade, I didn't think I'd ever hear from you again after that time I—"

"Yeah, I know. We were both drunk that night. It's water under the bridge now, and I have a favor to ask."

"Yeah, anything."

"I was given a case that might involve money laundering. Could you check it out for me on the down-low? You can't even let your leadership know about it, so please keep it under the table, okay?"

"Sure. How did you want to send it to me?"

Email wasn't secure, and I didn't trust the FBI network. "I'll overnight it to you with certified mail. Just text your address to this number I've called you on, okay?"

"Sure thing. And Jenna? I truly am sorry about that night."

"As I said, Hamilton, water under the bridge. But you would have had your world rocked."

He laughed. "Perhaps a rain check?"

"Help me without anyone finding out, and I'll owe you more than just a rain check."

"Deal."

I hung up and looked at the phone, remembering how handsome he had been in a nerdy and unsocial kind of way. It wasn't until I'd asked him out after graduation and got him drunk that he let loose.

I took Kimmel's hint, scanned copies of the laundering files through my father's tabletop scanner, and further studied Trevor Dark. According to his online bio, he graduated from Harvard Law School and had been a corporate attorney for many years before becoming CEO of Dark Enterprises. How did someone just do that?

He was on the cover of *GQ* and *Forbes*, and had been interviewed by many other news outlets. He was handsome with clean-cut wavy hair and a dark, shadowy Mediterranean look. Do I go to Dark Enterprises without Wilson's permission, and against the advice of Scelisi? I was initially curious just because it was located in a place where someone might have seen something, but after paging through this folder and being warned to stay away, I was even more curious.

Wilson hadn't called me, but fuck him. After the sloppiness I saw in those case folders, why would I want to follow or learn anything from him? Time to go a little rogue.

Chapter 9

The building that housed Dark Enterprises was far from a skyscraper, but it was at least fifteen stories high. Trevor Dark's offices comprised the top half, and the rest belonged to various small businesses.

The lobby resembled those of the most high-end hotels, from the marble floor with gold inlays to the beautiful chandeliers, expensive leather furniture, and live plants scattered throughout the monstrous room.

"Hi, I'm Agent Slade from the FBI," I told the guard at the front desk. "I'd like to see Mr. Dark, if he's available."

The man put an entire powdered sugar doughnut in his mouth, leisurely chewing it while staring at me. He didn't wipe away the white ring around his lips before leaning in to study my badge.

"Damn it, Josh, I said to be more professional," a female security officer said, stepping out from an adjacent counter. "I'm sorry, ma'am, he just started here. I'll call and check on his availability."

"Thank you." I put my badge away as Josh continued to gaze at me, chewing with that ring of white sugar on his face.

"Mr. Dark is available to see you," the woman said. "Please take this key card to the elevator over there, hold it against the touchpad, and press the top button marked P."

I grabbed the key card. "Got it. Thanks!"

As I turned around, I heard, "Josh, will you go to the restroom and wipe your face, or something? Come on, man, this is a professional building."

The elevator doors opened, revealing what appeared to be an Indian shrine with beautiful red and gold tapestries dressing the walls. One had families of elephants in some oasis. There was even a faint scent of lingering incense.

I placed the key card against the circular disk at the top of the panel, pressed P, and watched the doors gradually close. The entire ascent was relaxing, allowing me to appreciate the artwork. The music that piped in from above reminded me of what they'd always played at my father's favorite Indian restaurant.

When the doors opened, there was a woman across the way, wearing a Burberry plaid skirt and a cream-colored blouse. "Can I help you?" she asked.

"I'm sorry, this elevator is so relaxing I didn't want to leave it."

She smiled. "When Mr. Dark's wife had that designed, we all thought it strange, but everyone loves riding in that elevator now. Are you the agent here to meet with Mr. Dark?"

"Yes, Agent Jenna Slade." I showed her my badge.

"Okay, one minute. I'll let him know you're here."

She disappeared behind the wall bearing the Dark Enterprises logo in metallic gold letters. The lobby was simple, yet richly furnished with leather chairs, beautifully crafted marble-topped tables, and more live tropical plants.

"Mr. Dark will see you now. Right this way." The assistant escorted me down a hallway to the very end, where she opened the double doors and introduced me to the man inside. "Agent Jenna Slade, Mr. Dark."

"Agent Slade! Come on in."

Handsome fell short of summarizing Trevor Dark. In addition to a smile that could melt steel, he had ghostly gray eyes and dark wavy hair. He didn't need personality, although I'm sure he also had that to run a company like this.

"Um, hi, yes . . . I'm Agent Jenna Slade with the FBI." I showed him my badge.

"I trust you are who you say you are. Come in and have a seat."

He took a seat on a sofa, gesturing for me to sit beside him. The room was decorated from top to bottom with fabulous items from around the world, from paintings to vases, swords, antique muskets, and a small glass case covered in beautiful jewels.

As I crossed the carpet, my heart skipped a beat to find a woman with bright-red lipstick and a tight black dress standing in the room's far corner, blocked from view by the open door, almost as if she had purposefully hidden there. She was holding a cup of steaming coffee.

"Agent Slade, this is my wife, Sarah. Sarah Hanvey-Dark," he said with a wave of his arm.

"Good morning, Agent Slade," Sarah softly said, then sipped at the contents of her cup.

Sarah was stunningly beautiful, her long dark hair cascading down her back. She couldn't have been more than forty years old.

"I am here regarding a murder investigation across the street from this building," I said.

Trevor clasped his hands together and gazed deeply into my eyes. His captivating stare felt like it could pierce my soul, but I shook away the feeling and returned to my interview demeanor.

"Do you have any leads?" he asked intently.

Mrs. Dark just stared at me with a smile before taking another sip of her coffee.

"I can't say anything about the investigation, but considering your building has a glass wall across from that alley, I wondered if I could interview your employees. Perhaps they saw something odd over the past week or so."

"Of course, Jenna. May I call you Jenna?" his was voice smooth and captivating with a gaze on me like I'd seen of guys trying to pick me up at a bar years ago.

"Sure." Damn it, why did I say that? I usually preferred being called Agent Slade, but he had a natural charm.

I looked to Sarah, whose smile had slipped a bit, but she remained silent.

"Great!" said Trevor. "Jenna, I'll send out a building-wide message to cooperate. And I'll have security give you an all-access badge."

I usually never got this type of support. "That's great, Mr. Dark. I appreciate the help."

"All of it is yours . . . on one condition."

I knew there was a catch. "What might that be?"

"You must attend the Kids Across the Globe fundraiser we're having tomorrow night. It's a formal event, but being FBI, feel free to dress as you wish."

I frowned at his assumption that I had nothing elegant to wear. Sure, most FBI agents made little income, but I was single and could afford elegance . . . if I wanted to. "Why would you want me to attend this event?"

"You are lovely, Jenna, and I like to bring as much beauty into my affairs as possible."

I rarely got uncomfortable at a guy hitting on me, but his wife stood in the same room made me a tad uneasy. Something told me he was looking for an affair of another type and his wife didn't say a word. "Where is it?"

"It will be held in our lobby downstairs Friday night at 7:00 p.m. I'll be looking for you, Jenna."

He stood up, and I instinctively stood as well. He placed his hand on the small of my back and walked me to the door.

"It was delightful meeting you, Agent Slade," Sarah said as we passed. "Do let us know if we can be of any further help."

"Thank you, Mrs. Dark."

"That would be Mrs. Hanvey-Dark, my dear," she corrected and sipped her coffee again.

"Good evening, Jenna," Trevor said.

As I walked down the hallway, I looked back to see him watching me. I didn't know what he was watching, as I wore my typical pants suit with a jacket.

What the hell just happened? I thought when I got to the lobby.

"Can I help you, Agent Slade?"

The receptionist broke my confused contemplation. "Huh? Oh, um, no, I'm good. Although, actually, who might I see about getting a building-access list and entry/exit records?"

"You would need to contact our chief of security." She typed on her computer and wrote a phone number down on the top sheet of a beautifully monogrammed notepad.

"Thank you."

Back in the elevator, I stared at the family of elephants.

How had he done that to me? Sure, he was attractive and his voice was captivating, but damn it, I was a trained field agent. I could do better than that, and he was so much older. And what was up with him flirting while his wife watched?

Chapter 10

When I arrived at the office, Baxter and Porter were sitting together on Wilson's desk. They quieted as soon as they saw me approach.

"What's the matter? Can't talk when I'm around?" I asked.

"Don't you have a burglar to catch? It looks like you need an academy refresher," Baxter said with a chuckle. Porter smiled at me before looking down at the file in his hands. I understood why he didn't want to acknowledge our connection, but that didn't stop my frustration at his support of the little hobbit.

"Trust me. I'm on it. Where's Wilson?" It was time for him to fully update me on this case.

Baxter replied, "Downstairs, trying to get info on the Jane Doe Blonde Number Two you stumbled on a few days ago."

"Hey, Porter, what do you have going on with this investigation . . . or anything?" I asked, wanting to jostle him out of his apparent attempt to ignore me.

"Assisting Wilson, like the rest of us are," Baxter replied.

Porter gave a curt nod without responding . . . Whoa. Did he even make eye contact?

"Whatever. Does he need special permission to speak?" I mumbled before heading off to see what Wilson was up to down in the basement. Based on Dr. Jefferies's weird reaction to mentioning Wilson during our last conversation, I decided to sneak up on him and take the stairs so he wouldn't hear me get off the elevator.

With some steady pressure, I opened the heavy steel door just enough for me to pass through and made sure it shut securely behind me with a minimal click. As soon as I entered, the pungent scent of hospital and death filled the air.

A hushed conversation resonated from the end of the hall. A locked storage room stood between me and the examination room, with no avenue of escape except toward Dr. Jefferies's office or going back to the stairwell.

Careful not to draw any attention, I eased forward.

"I've done what you've told me to do. Now where is my reassignment?" Dr. Jefferies's voice was stressed and desperate.

"There isn't one open yet, so in the meantime, continue to do as you're told and everything will be okay." That was Wilson's voice.

"Have you been using me this entire time? I thought I meant something to you."

"Like Slade meant something to you? You still mean something to me, and if you know what's good for you, you'll continue to mean something to me."

What the hell? Was Wilson blackmailing her? And did "Slade" mean my father? Did Dr. Jefferies have a relationship with my father?

"Is everything erased with Blondie out there?" Wilson continued.

"You know I can't do it from here, but it's taken care of. So, yes, nobody will ever find out about anything we did here. The tests will show alcohol like all the others."

"Good work, Becky. See how easy this can be?"

"Stop it. I don't want you near me anymore. I just want to move on with my life and forget about this mess—and you." Suddenly, she cried out. "Ow! That hurts."

"You obey, or else someone at the Bureau may get an anonymous tip about what *you* did here. Hell, a senior officer uncovering a corrupt medical examiner could even mean a promotion. What would happen then?"

Her sniffles stirred something within me, and I could no longer idly sit by.

"Dr. Jefferies? It's Agent Slade," I called out in the opposite direction to appear farther away, then walked toward her office.

Dr. Jefferies was in her chair facing Wilson, while Wilson backed away, adjusting his belt and smoothing out his hair.

"Oh, there you are," I said. "Agent Wilson, I didn't know you were down here."

"What are you doing here, Slade?" Wilson asked, appearing to have just stood up, using his hand to ensure every strand of his slicked-back hair was in place.

"I came down to find out how the autopsy was coming along on the Jane Doe I found."

Dr. Jefferies walked out of the office to the desk in the exam room. She held out a folder. "Here it is."

"I'll take that," Wilson said, pulling it out of her hands. "Know your place, Slade." He scanned through the folder and looked at Becky. "Good job, Doctor. Come on, Slade, let's not waste the good doctor's time."

Becky's frown held every indication of nervousness or fear, but the alarm bells were still ringing in my head. I wanted to stay and ask about my father, but decided to do so another time.

I followed Wilson to the elevator with my eyes on the floor, trying to digest what I'd heard.

The distinguishable ding of the elevator sounded, and we got on.

"Why didn't you take the elevator down?" Wilson asked. He must have noticed the ding too.

I thought fast. "I always try to take the stairs to stay in shape. You should try it."

"I'm perfectly fit, thank you," he replied as the doors opened again.

"I'd like you to reconsider visiting Dark."

Baxter was still at Wilson's desk. "I see she found you."

"Yeah, she found me. And I said, stay away from Dark Enterprises. They have nothing to do with this case."

Damn it, he was suspicious now. Maybe I'd hold off on telling him.

Kimmel passed through the open space and barked, "Slade! My office. Now!"

I tried to remember what I'd done wrong this time, but I couldn't think of anything.

"Looks like your time here might be up sooner than we thought," Wilson snickered. Baxter joined in with a grin, but Porter kept silent, still avoiding eye contact. I guess I should look into other options for de-stressing.

As soon as I entered, Agent Kimmel slammed the door behind me.

"I don't know what I did wrong this—"

"I slammed the door for dramatic effect, just as I'm going to do with waving my arms. The report is back on the photographs you delivered, and I want you to pick them up. I'll let you know where to meet me afterward. Don't come back here with them. Have you made heads or tails of that folder on Dark Enterprises yet?"

"I'm still studying it. I did meet with Mr. Dark at his building, and he granted me access to interview the employees to see if they witnessed anything." I didn't tell her about the ball, or that Hamilton was looking over the audit documents as well. I wanted to be sure what I gained was pertinent first.

"Okay, just let me know if you find anything of significance. Maybe I can kick it back to Miami HQ if it has something juicy enough." Kimmel continued loudly, "Do you understand? Now get out of my office!"

I fought off a smile at the theatrics but painted a somber expression as I reemerged.

"It's okay, Slade. There's always a need for crossing guards. Right, Wilson?" Baxter said, trying to show off. Porter shook his head and pretended to be reading a document.

As I started to reply, I noticed that Wilson's squinted eye was trying to scan me like an x-ray machine. He was unquestionably suspicious.

I had to stay strong and not give him anything further to be suspicious about.

My head was foggy. Had my father been involved with Wilson and Dr. Jefferies.

Chapter 11

The last time I had needed to dress up was for a friend's wedding. Unfortunately, the bachelorette party had included three bridesmaids and the wedding was canceled, leaving me with a strapless burgundy number. Still, I wanted something different, something that boasted beautiful yet strong.

I drove down to Grand Avenue, headed for an elite boutique where my friend and I had once tried on bridesmaid dresses. Once the manager realized we had no intention of buying anything, she asked us to leave. Everything there was overpriced, anyway. But with the amount of money my father had left me, I could splurge a little.

As I walked up, the clerk unlocked the door. "Welcome, I'm Caitlin. How can I help you?" She had a cheery disposition and a smile that could force the nastiest of trolls to smile back. Her black-and-white pencil skirt and blue satin blouse had to have cost a fortune.

"Thank you. I'm looking for a formal gown for a ball. Something beautiful and strong."

"Fabulous. Would this be for the Dark Enterprises fundraiser?"

"Why, yes, it is. How did you know?"

"Oh, sweetie, many ladies have been here in the past few weeks to prepare for that ball. It's a great annual revenue generator for our store. I'm sure we have something that will work for you. You're a size six, right?"

"Yes, but I only have an hour to find something."

"Great, then let's get started. Follow me to the dressing room."

I stood in the dressing room, weighing the pros and cons of each evening gown Caitlin picked. A cobalt-blue dress with Renaissance-style frills and a bustle caught my eye. I rarely giggle, but it slipped out as I imagined myself as a secret agent for a king somewhere four hundred years ago, with modern weapons beneath my billowing skirts.

Next Caitlin handed me a deep-red silk dress with spaghetti straps. It was slinky, and I hesitated before pulling it over my head. When I gazed into the mirror, I was shocked to see a woman I hardly recognized. The material hugged every curve of my body. I let my hair down from its high ponytail, watching as it cascaded around my shoulders and lit my face with a joyful glow. I exuded confidence.

"And with your bust, you can tuck in those straps to wear it strapless, if you like," Caitlin said as she pulled them from my shoulders and tucked them under my arms.

The shimmer of the fabric captivated me, as did my figure. I would receive a lot of attention wearing this dress. I wanted to look good, but not that good.

After I hung the red dress up with a sigh, Caitlin brought me a long black dress. The mock turtleneck showed my shoulders, and the narrow opening from neck to belly showed off a modest amount of skin. The rest also fit me like a glove.

Caitlin stood back, biting her lip. "If this isn't the one, then I have nothing for you."

"It's perfect." I twisted to see myself from every possible angle. Now came the tough pill to swallow. "How much is it?"

"That dress is $2,200."

My teeth and lips clenched, realizing that I'd never spent so much on clothing before, but I was confident I'd wear this dress again sometime.

"How much is the red one?"

Caitlin winced. "That one is $4,300."

I tried to hide my hard swallow. Ten years ago, I would have never imagined spending more than two hundred bucks on a dress—but what good is having that inheritance if I didn't use it?

I took a deep breath. "I'll take it."

"Great, I'll wrap it up for you."

"I mean, I'll take both this one and the red one. I've never seen myself look as good as in that red dress, and it's time I did something for myself."

As I drove through the suburban area where Kimmel's informant, Holly, lived, I was trying to understand my dad's relationship with Dr. Jefferies.

The door opened before I could even knock. The same woman stepped out, scanned the area, handed me the large manila envelope, and without a word, stepped back into the house.

I returned to my car, set the envelope on the passenger seat, and drove home.

My heart skipped a beat when I saw a black sports car turn three cars behind me. Was it following me?

I shook it out of my head and continued to drive home. As I turned to my neighborhood, I saw another black car not far behind me again. This couldn't be a coincidence.

Without a second thought, my foot slammed onto the gas pedal, jerking the car forward and screeching around a block. I wanted this bastard to either chase me, or I'd try to get behind it, but when I rounded the block again, no sign of the car.

It had to be real—it must have been right there—but now it was gone.

Was I losing my mind? I drove erratically around the neighborhood, searching desperately for that same black car.

When I returned, I set my two investment dresses in their boxes on the kitchen table and went directly to my father's office, impatient as a kid at Christmas. I wanted inside that envelope in the worst way. But a stamped seal covered the adhered flap. Damn it! If I opened this, Kimmel would know for sure.

I flipped on the desk lamp, turned it so the bulb faced me, and held the envelope to the light, but I couldn't see anything. I guess I needed to join the CIA to learn how to break into an envelope like this.

I threw it on the desk and walked to get a bump of scotch. The first time my father had let me try it at fifteen, I nearly threw up. Since his passing, I'd gradually acquired a taste for it but realized there were many better brands than he had in the house. Although I didn't come in his office often, I figured when I did, I should at least have a brand I liked.

The warm, oak smoothness was just what I needed. As I sipped, I unhurriedly paged through the pictures on the end table, sliding them around. I took another sip and looked down at the bottle, wondering how many times he'd poured from that bottle when he was stressed with his job.

Kimmel hadn't actually told me not to open the envelope.

Grabbing a letter opener from my father's desk drawer, I wiggled it into the top of the envelope and paused, worried about whether I was making the right decision and analyzing the repercussions. A second later, the seam sliced open.

The documents were pictures of the Jane Does at various activities. College parties, cheerleading, dinners, picnics, and even a formal event, perhaps a wedding. They were from social media sources with a name for each.

Zahra Kaplan was a Middle Eastern-looking woman with beautiful blue eyes. There were several pictures of her with family and friends in a formal gown at some ball. Another photo was of her in a swimming suit, surrounded by friends at the beach. None of these pictures were selfies.

She was Jane Doe Brunette.

But how had all her records gotten erased, and why was there a trust created in her name?

The following photo had the name Emily Hawkins on the bottom.

I removed the paper clip that held the photographs of Emily together and compared them to the picture of Jane Doe Blonde #2. They, too, were a match.

I suspected that whoever I'd given the photos to had done a global facial recognition search. I knew there were special groups in the FBI and CIA that could do this. Why didn't Kimmel just have one of those organizations get this information?

I looked through the envelope, but there were no pictures of Jane Doe Redhead or the original Jane Doe Blonde.

I thought about the whispers I'd overheard between Dr. Jefferies and Wilson, and I couldn't help but think they might be involved in guaranteeing certain details were never put in those case folders, but who else would be involved?

Did Kimmel expect to find this?

I tossed back the remaining swallow of scotch in my glass and thought about that key my father had. Did he have a vault in Europe with cash, or gold, or maybe the secret to JFK's assassination? It could be almost anything, but any vault would surely contain something significant to use one of the most secure sites in the world—or so I would assume.

These photos would be key evidence in this case, and I had the only copy. I had to save it all on something. My father had given me a thumb drive containing family photos before he died, and told me to keep it in the music box he'd given me when I was young. I placed it in the copier and set the photos on the tray to scan onto the thumb drive.

Then I booted up my father's computer again and searched through his bank and credit card statements from the year before he died. Perhaps there was some sign of where he'd gone all those times he traveled.

An hour went by, and other than drink charges at Stella's, a local bar where retired FBI agents hung out, there wasn't much. He didn't have any debt, but he did have a $50,000 credit limit, and the card was still active. I sat back, curious about how someone on an FBI salary, albeit a senior agent, could have such an impressive line of credit. Of course, he had substantial savings from his parents' inheritance and life insurance, but it was another piece of confusion. And why was his credit card still active? It should have been closed out after he'd died eight years ago.

Finally, I found a Delta Airlines charge of $7,000 and a charge to the Hotel Schweizerhof that occurred a couple of years before he died. My fingers hurriedly queued up the hotel on Google and saw it was in Switzerland. I didn't remember him ever going to Switzerland, although he kidded about skiing in the Alps . . . or was he kidding?

Switzerland definitely had private banks the key might belong to.

I scanned more records, but there were no other charges to either of those entities.

After being on hold for fifteen minutes, someone at Delta answered. I presented myself as FBI Agent Slade, but they wouldn't release any information without an order from a judge.

Hearing a knock at the front door, I hastily compiled the photos into the envelope, placed it in the top drawer of my father's desk, and walked down the hall.

"Scelisi! What brings you by this evening?"

He wasn't wearing a suit jacket as he normally did, and carried no service weapon. His eyes were low and concerning. "Jenna, I believe you might be in danger," he said as he pushed past me.

"Come on in," I said, making my sarcasm obvious while gesturing with my hand. "What danger am I in?"

"I believe you're researching things that will concern many powerful people."

"How do you know what I'm researching?"

His blank stare at me was even more suspicious. So many thoughts immediately flashed through my mind, and all of them involved someone spying on me.

"You asked earlier about Dark Enterprises, so I'm assuming you're researching them," he said.

I guess I could accept that, but why now?

"Jenna, I need that key. It's the only thing that can save you and many others," he insisted.

I maintained my composure. "I really don't know what key you're referring to."

His eyes went from somber to anger, his forehead wrinkled with impatience. "Jenna, we don't have time for games. I have confident knowledge of your finding the key, and I need it."

I backed away a few steps. "What does this alleged key open?"

"I believe your father was onto something big, and he knew he was in trouble, so he either hid files or a hard drive somewhere in a secure location. That key may be the link to this information."

My curiosity swiftly ballooned to anger as I realized my father's trusted partner—someone who I'd trusted my entire life—had lied to me. "Did my father kill himself, or was he killed for this key?"

He paused and stepped closer to me. I moved backward, keeping a cautious distance away. "It's not as simple as that, Jenna. Your father was found hanging by a rope, and there was no evidence of a struggle, and a note was on the table next to him, so that is what the autopsy report cited."

"Who did the autopsy?" Deep down, I knew the answer but wanted to be wrong.

"Dr. Becky Jefferies."

I stepped back in horror. So many dots were connecting.

"I need you to leave," I said as I opened the door.

"This is the big leagues. You're in danger having that key. It could be the only thing to uncover the truth about your father's death."

"I told you, I don't know what key you mean. Now leave!"

Scelisi stopped in the doorway and turned to me. "I would never harm you, Jenna."

"Are you spying on me?" I blurted.

"I don't want to see you hurt," he said. "If you find the key, please provide it." provide the key if you find it."

After he left, I slammed the door shut so hard that a portrait of my mother fell from the entryway wall. I ran my fingers through my hair, trying to digest what I had just learned. Then I reset my mother's portrait on the wall and straightened it, taking a deep, calming breath. Then I returned to my father's office and opened the top desk drawer.

Shit! The envelope was gone.

The window was unlocked, but the alarm hadn't warned me that the window had opened. I looked at the copier and sighed in relief— the thumb drive remained in the slot.

Enraged, I opened the window and looked outside.

"Office window is open," the alarm voice bellowed from the hallway.

The pins holding the screen in place were not secure. Why hadn't the alarm given the same warning then as it did just now? The sensor appeared untouched.

Had Scelisi been distracting me while someone broke in?

I walked to the copier, removed the thumb drive, and placed it in my father's computer.

The small circle icon spun around as I waited impatiently.

There were three files on the thumb drive. I opened the recent one and sighed in relief as the photos appeared. What was in the other files? I opened the one labeled "Family Photos," and after a few seconds, I was looking at thumbnail pictures of my life. I took a deep breath and promised myself I'd return to this. I closed it and looked at the next file labeled "Remember."

I nearly cried when I saw the nursery rhyme, Hickory Dickory Dock. It was my favorite nursery rhyme when I was little, as my father would hold me upside down and swing me like the pendulum in a clock. There were more verses, but I only liked the mouse and the monkey.

My gaze went to the corkboard, only to stop—it wasn't wise to place my research and analysis on that board right now if my house could be broken into so easily.

I reached for the clip on my belt that sat on the desk, pulled it out of the magazine holder, removed the top bullet, and pulled out the key. "What do you fit into?"

The wall clock chimed, and the time on the computer screen displayed 6:00 p.m.

I needed to get ready for the ball.

Chapter 12

As I passed through the security screening at Dark Enterprises, the alarm went off.

"Miss, I'll need you to stand aside."

My gun was detected, no doubt.

I reached inside my matching black clutch and showed my badge to the security guard.

"We have our own security, miss. We won't need any more. We can't let you in with that."

"What's going on here?" An older man with a white crew cut, matching well-trimmed beard, and a black suit appeared. His earpiece indicated he was security.

"The FBI agent here has her service weapon, but we don't need any further security."

I showed my badge again. He leaned in, looked at a list of names, and said, "It's okay. She's a guest of Mr. Dark. We can let her through."

"Thank you," I said and put my badge away.

An attendant passed me a brochure as the senior security representative headed back toward the more extensive section of the gala.

The pamphlet discussed where the money gathered tonight would be going. The lobby displayed pictures of kids from around the world who had been helped by this fundraiser, along influential lawmakers and ministers who'd donated handsomely. Other images displayed lorries carrying grains for third-world nations, water supply systems in the process of being built, and doctors providing healthcare treatment to those who otherwise wouldn't have any.

I was in a receiving line, waiting to get into the primary part of the event, when I heard Trevor Dark's voice. He and his wife were welcoming guests at the entrance. When our eyes met, even thirty feet away, I was mesmerized by his captivating eyes, which were like bait to a fish. My fear was that there was a hook somewhere.

Crap! I snapped back in line. Why was my body responding this way? Of course, he was handsome and wealthy, but I was here to investigate *his* company.

"Jenna! I'm so glad you could make it. And my, you are absolutely stunning in that dress. Don't you think, love?" Trevor asked his wife.

Mrs. Hanvey-Dark replied, "Yes, very lovely, dear." Her eyes scanned me from my heels to my hair. I held back my grin. She hadn't expected me to look like this tonight.

"Thank you. This looks like a fabulous event," I said, not

knowing what to say. I'd been to a few weddings, but never something of this brilliance.

"Sueann!" Trevor called to a woman in conversation with a gentleman in a black tuxedo with a blue-and-yellow sash. "Sueann, I want you to meet Agent Jenna Slade of the FBI. She is our special guest this evening. Will you show her around and explain more of what we do?"

Sueann? As in the trust account name? Surely it was a coincidence.

Sueann came over and extended her hand. "Good evening, I'm Sueann. It would be a pleasure to show you around."

Trevor checked me out before turning his attention elsewhere. *Maybe I should have worn the red dress.*

After taking two flutes of champagne from a server's tray, Sueann walked alongside me.

"That dress looks amazing on you, and your hair is stunning," she said. After a pause, she added, "I must find out who did it for you!"

I didn't have the heart to tell her I learned to do a chignon low bun from a YouTube video.

"Thank you. I was hoping it wasn't too much," I said, trying to make some small talk as I scanned the room. A few hundred people of many nationalities were gathered in small groups, talking and some laughing.

"You are so beautiful. And so young. How old are you?" she asked.

"Twenty-eight."

"I wish I were twenty-eight again, but I'm doing pretty good for forty-five."

I stood back a moment to look at her. She had perfect cheekbones, shoulder-length dirty-blonde hair, and a body most models would die for.

"There's no way you're forty-five. If I had to guess, I'd say early thirties . . . maybe."

She laughed. "You're so kind. I'm glad the expensive plastic surgeon does well, and a personal trainer helps me keep my figure."

"What's your role in Dark Enterprises?" I asked.

She pondered briefly. "Well, I was once a government program manager in Boston, where I oversaw billions of dollars in government weapon system programs. Some of the programs were contracted with Dark Enterprises." She downed half of the champagne in her glass. "But over the last few years, Trevor and I have become very close. Very, very close. The kind of close where I may be fired if anyone found out." She took another sip of her champagne.

I whispered, "Are you having an affair with him?"

"An affair would involve sneaking around a spouse. His wife knows of our relationship, so I don't have to feel too guilty. Besides, he's making me very wealthy for following him."

"How long did you work with the government?" I asked and took a sip of the bubbly. Then I looked at it in surprise. Wow. I'd never had champagne this fabulous before.

"I worked there for twenty-six years. Four years short of a full retirement. From the age of nineteen, I did what I was told, grew through the ranks of program management, and became a senior manager just to have some thirty-something millennial become my boss. I went volcanic. I nearly destroyed my office in a rage. That was when Dark offered me a dream life. Even as his mistress, it's a life I could never have had on my own."

I discreetly raised my eyebrows while sipping a generous portion of liquid courage. Too much information was an understatement, yet my intrigue got the better of me. "Does he provide some type of allowance, or something?"

A server walked up to us with two new flutes.

"Even better . . ." Sueann downed the rest of her bubbly, grabbed mine, and replaced ours with filled glasses. "He has given me access to a bank account and trust fund worth millions, and all I have to do is always be available when he calls. He showers me with expensive gifts, such as this diamond necklace, and provides me with a much more extravagant lifestyle than I ever could have imagined."

I gazed at her three-tiered necklace with three princess-cut diamonds, a layer of two under that, and a gorgeous teardrop diamond under that. The light reflected brilliantly on the beautiful stones. But my body felt like it had turned to stone. Sueann . . . she was the person associated with the trust fund.

"Are you all right?" she inquired.

I regained my composure. "I'm good. I rarely drink so much,

and it's suddenly hitting me."

Sueann laughed, twined her arm inside mine, and guided us around the event. The crystal chandeliers cast subtle rainbows in every direction, decorating the large portraits of children in Africa being helped by Dark's supply trucks of food and medicine.

I didn't want to drink too much, but Sueann kept insisting. We were on our fourth glass, and I was beyond tipsy. I felt like I was in college again, drunk and looking for some sensual satisfaction. I absurdly found every man in the room desirable, even the large server with scars on his face. Unfortunately, even if I called Porter to come over, I was no longer sure he would show up.

"Have you been in Dark's room yet?" Sueann whispered.

"Um, no. What's in Dark's room?"

"It's called a blackout room. You remove your clothing before entering, and whatever happens in the darkness . . . happens."

"Are you kidding?" I called out more loudly than I wanted. A few nearby eyes turned.

"Shh."

I whispered, "You're kidding, right?" I enjoyed sex, but a thousand scenarios flashed through my mind, most of them frightening. Yet for some strange reason, my core heated up at the very thought of what might happen in a room like that. "Why would you tell this to someone you just met?" I could have asked more delicately, but I felt emboldened by the champagne.

Sueann stopped, her eyes apologetically soft. "I'm sorry. I

thought the reason Dark asked me to spend time with you was to introduce you to that room. You are very beautiful, and he looks for women to enjoy themselves in the room. I was instantly comfortable with you, and—I'm so very sorry if I was too presumptuous."

I had to think fast. I needed to smooth out this discussion and stay engaged with her. It was too coincidental she had the same name as the trust fund.

"It's okay. One never knows where the night takes us."

"Right," she said, raising her glass. I clinked mine and took a drink.

A Mediterranean-looking man with a blue sash and two medals on his chest walked by. His cologne attacked my nostrils like the pheromones of a Greek god. My heart raced and my mouth went dry—an instant, overpowering desire for this stranger hit me like a tidal wave. I had never felt such unexpected lust before, not even for Porter. His broad shoulders were like mountains I needed to climb.

I asked Sueann who he was in a whisper. She informed me he was Donte, from a well-to-do Italian family with many political ties. He had diplomatic status on his visits to the US. She paused and added, "He is quite easy on the eyes."

"Yes," I breathed softly. "He is indeed."

"I'm confident he'll be in Dark's room later. You should join us. It's an experience like you've never had."

I bet it is.

Another server approached us with flutes—this time a woman,

perhaps in her twenties. Sueann swapped out our glasses again. I wanted to chug it and grab another, but I needed to keep any wits I had left. I felt euphoric, as though I were gliding on a cloud, and my desire for release grew.

Sueann continued in a low voice, "You can say no . . . if you want, but you don't know who is in the room. It could be a man, or a woman, or both. You only have your touch, smell, and hearing to help you navigate. It's more exciting than you could ever imagine. The only light is the exit sign, so you know where to leave. The experience and sensations are beyond incredible."

I looked down at the floor until I could get my composure. "That does sound interesting, but do you know who these others are in the room?"

After checking to make sure no one was nearby, she whispered, "There have been times when Trevor thanked me for taking care of his guests, so I imagine some are the very men and women in this room."

I couldn't help but look at the room with new eyes. There was a mix of attractive and not-so-attractive men from many parts of the world.

"Here's my number." Sueann pulled out a business card from her cleavage. "You must come visit me sometime. Dark usually joins me there, but lately he's been all wrapped up in his job. It really helps reduce sexual energy. I'm so charged up now. I can't wait for that room to open tonight!"

"Wait, you're going there tonight?" I asked.

"Of course. It's a big event for Trevor, and I want him to be pleased while satisfying my own needs as well."

The alcohol scrambled my thoughts, but I tried to concentrate. A room like that would be the perfect setting to murder someone, and no one would be the wiser. I needed Sueann to gain my trust, but I wasn't sure how to accomplish that, other than continuing personal talk like two sisters. "Aren't you worried about, you know . . . getting an infection, or worse?"

"Yes, I've thought about it. But Trevor assured me that everyone is safe, and if I did get anything, he would take care of me."

What she said almost seemed like something a teenager would say, not a grown woman. I needed to change the subject.

"What about Mrs. Hanvey-Dark?" I gestured toward Sarah, who was speaking and laughing with a group of men wearing expensive Armani suits. She glanced at us briefly before returning to her conversation.

"You mean Sarah? Yes, she's very particular about her name being mentioned exactly as it is. But other than that, she doesn't say much to me."

"Has she ever gone in the Dark Room?"

"I don't know. I see some women in the locker room removing their clothes, but I've never seen her."

"There's a locker room?"

"Sure, that way we can shower afterward. It's a pretty classy event."

I struggled not to squint as I tried to understand how any of it was classy.

"Do you know those men who Dark is talking to?" I asked, and then it hit me. "Never mind, I think I know."

It was Vice President Brandon and his son, Chet. The vice president and Sarah walked off to talk alone, a secret service agent standing nearby, but the vice president's son remained talking to Dark. When they looked toward us, Sueann blushed and smiled back, giving a small wave of her fingers to say hello. Chet nodded as Dark whispered something in his ear. Regarding his Dark Room, no doubt.

"Have you already been with the vice president's son?" I tried to whisper without displaying concern.

"I may have," she said, continuing to smile. "He flirted with me, and hinted that he would be in the Dark Room, but I can't confirm I was actually with him, if you know what I mean. I think I heard his voice tell me to do something, but I couldn't be sure. It's the benefit for his special guests. They get their pleasure with attractive women, and no one knows."

"How do they know who they're with?" I found it strange that all these men would stumble around aimlessly in a room full of people.

"Oh, I think they have infrared glasses. It's just the women who can't see, but it's okay. I like the mystery behind it."

"What about that woman who died the other day across the street? Did you know her?"

"I heard about it. That's so sad, and scary it was so nearby."

"Does the name Emily ring a bell?"

"I knew an Emily who did what I do to help Trevor. She had been with him longer and traveled to Europe with him. I heard she moved to Greece with her trust fund. I was so envious, and I can't wait to follow in her footsteps."

I feared for her life, but telling her what I'd found might cause Dark to do something drastic. Perhaps I'd follow up with her in a few days in a more discreet setting.

I looked at a portrait of Dark handing sacks of grain to villagers somewhere. "Are you the only arm candy Dark has?"

She took a long sip of her champagne. "He doesn't tell me such things, and I don't ask. I'm content with the life he gives me, and if he has another woman, then I'm okay with that. Tell me, what's it like to be an FBI agent?" Sueann turned toward the violinist in the corner of the room—obviously, Trevor's other mistresses was a subject she didn't want to pursue.

"To tell you the truth . . ."

"Agent Slade."

Mrs. Hanvey-Dark had appeared with the vice president and his secret service agent.

"Vice President Brandon, let me introduce you to one of Miami's finest FBI agents. Agent Jenna Slade," Mrs. Hanvey-Dark said.

"Good evening, Agent Slade, this is my son, Chet."

The vice president's son winked at me and smiled. I tried to hold back my disdain and the ever-growing vomit that wanted to rise from my stomach.

The vice president narrowed his eyes in apparent thought. "Do you have any relation to Charlie Slade?"

"He was my father."

"He was a good man. He worked for me a while back. I'm sure you'll do well in the Bureau."

As one of his entourages pulled him away, I stared at him, puzzled. My father had never mentioned anything about working for the vice president. Mrs. Hanvey-Dark followed, giving me a final cool smile.

The vice president's son whispered to Sueann, "Will I find you in the room later?"

She smiled. "I'll be there. Whether you'll find me is up to you."

"Will you be bringing this heavenly delight?" he asked.

They both looked at me, and he was already undressing me with his eyes. He didn't even hide his creepy disposition.

"I don't know. I've been trying to reel her in."

"The chance to get both of you would help me influence some wonderful investments in your favor. Maybe a role in a nongovernment organization and make some real money?"

"I'll think about it," I replied, mostly to stop us from continuing down this degrading path.

"You do that, and it might benefit your career too."

My body was torn between running out of the building or following the next attractive man into the restroom for a quick fix. The internal tug-of-war was something I'd never experienced before.

I glanced across the room to see the tall Italian man talking to two older men wearing blue sashes. Suddenly, he locked his eyes with me. Like a high school girl, my face warmed with embarrassment. I sipped my drink and returned to Sueann.

"Dark's clients come in from around the world for these events." Sueann pulled me in, her arm in mine, and pointed at a portrait. "Some say there's more than grain in those sacks," she whispered.

"If Dark took you away from your professional career, and his wife is networking with him among clients, where does that leave you?" No sooner than I said it, I wanted to apologize.

"Dark is good to me. I stay now because he makes me happy, and I enjoy the lifestyle he gives me."

"I'm sorry, Sueann, I'm . . . I'm just confused. This is all so new to me." My curiosity was on overload, and now I needed to figure out how to keep her from being next on the dumpster list. "Will you excuse me for a moment? I need to use the powder room. I'll be right back."

"Oh, I need to go as well."

Great.

The women's restroom was also impressive, with a sofa and

chairs, and an attendant to hand out towels and clean the stalls. I sat down, opened my clutch to take out my phone, and noted down everything Sueann had told me. I also wanted to take pictures of those men in the expensive suits.

When I opened the stall door, Mrs. Hanvey-Dark was in front of the mirror. I looked around . . . there was no Sueann.

"Are you enjoying the evening, Agent?"

"Agent Slade." *I just had to.* "And yes, I'm enjoying it very much." I tried to maintain my composure, but the four-plus glasses of champagne had hit me more than expected.

"I imagine you don't get to attend too many of these events in your line of work," she said while patting her nose with a pad. "That's a fabulous dress. I suspect you purchased it at Caitlin's. She's quite expensive for an agent's salary." She put her makeup in her clutch and looked at me, smiling. "I do hope you enjoy the rest of your evening." She walked toward the door and paused. "Don't feel the need to make a donation. We're simply happy to have you here with us," she said before leaving.

The immediate word that came to mind was "Bitch!" Sure, I didn't make much money at my job, but that was kind of cold.

"What a cold-hearted—"

"You said it," Sueann said as she opened the door to another stall.

"You were still here!" I laughed.

"Of course, I was about to flush when I heard her voice. I didn't want to make it too obvious I was here."

"Do you think she followed us in here?"

"I don't try to think much of anything with her. Now you see why Dark prefers to take me traveling instead."

When we walked outside, we ran into the man in the blue sash. His cologne filled my senses, and all rational thought left my mind. My only desire was to have him against me.

"*Scusate*," he said in a deep voice. I could make out every facial hair in his evening shadow and yearned for his bristles against my skin.

"Oh, sorry, I only speak English."

He smiled. "My Italian often just flows out of me."

There was no subtlety to my ogling, and I had no guilt in doing so. I wished everyone here would leave so we could be alone for an hour or two.

"I see you enjoy the champagne . . . yes?"

I bit my lower lip and nodded. I could barely contain myself anymore. I wanted to throw caution to the wind and ask him to go off with me alone—anywhere. I looked at Sueann, who gave me a wink.

He leaned in close, his whiskers lightly brushing against my cheek. The heat from his breath was electrifying. "Perhaps you would prefer to come back to my hotel room, where it is little more privat?"

If he threw me over his shoulder right now, I wouldn't resist. A loss of words was the least of my concerns as I fought off having an orgasm right there. In my tipsy state, I would need to take a taxi home anyhow, so why not indulge?

Without removing my gaze from his deep blue eyes, I handed my glass to Sueann. "Sueann . . . I appreciate everything tonight, but I believe I'll be leaving now."

"I'm sure your night will be fabulous as well," Sueann said. "I hope to see you again soon . . . and call me anytime. Let's get together for lunch."

"Yes, I'd like that," I replied without looking at her.

Mr. Delicious placed his hand on the small of my back and escorted me toward the entrance. My heart wanted to leap from my chest, and every few seconds, my mind said, "Don't," only to be beaten down by my subconscious animal within.

"Since I'm going back to your room, might I at least know your name?"

"Of course. My name is Donte Bario. My father donates millions to this organization, and I come here to represent him, and sometimes the Italian government."

"Who are you representing right now?"

He caressed my arm. "Tonight, I only think about you."

"Jenna?"

Shit, Scelisi! I'd never seen him in a tuxedo before, and I barely recognized him. He wore an earpiece. I suspect he was part of the security for the event, or the vice president.

"Jenna, what are you doing here? You shouldn't be here," he whispered.

"Mr. Dark invited me. Why are you here? Did you come to distract me so you could have someone sneak into my house again?"

"I'm on detail for the vice president. What are you talking about?"

"Oh, like my father was, and I never knew." I thought better than to say any more, especially since I was distinctly slurring.

"Jenna, you need to leave."

"I'm taking the lovely lady away right now," Donte said, patting my arm.

Scelisi looked between us. "Jenna, I'll take you home so you're safe."

"Frankly, I'll take my chances with Donte." I looked up to the chiseled face of the Mediterranean god and said, "Let's go, Donte."

We pushed past Scelisi and continued walking.

"If any harm comes to her, Bario . . ."

Hearing that, the agent part of me fleetingly broke through. "How do you know Scelisi?" I asked Donte.

"He performs some tasks now and then. Helps make shipping go smoother."

As we walked outside, I tried to file that away in my foggy database. He handed the valet some cash in exchange for his keys.

"This way," Donte said.

We walked down an aisle of ridiculously expensive cars, and the lights flashed on an Aston Martin.

"This is your car?" I asked, seeing perhaps five years of my salary represented in this one piece of luxury.

"This is my American car. The one I have in Italy is far better. America puts too many rules on car making."

He opened the passenger door and helped me inside. In the mirror, I saw Scelisi by the entrance, making a call on his cell phone as he watched us leave.

Chapter 13

Donte's large, strong hand on my leg on the way to the hotel sent shivers through my body. I kept looking down at it, wanting it to move along my smooth skin, but it didn't.

"Would you consider yourself a dangerous man?" I asked.

The city's lights were flashing by so quickly that I couldn't tell where we were.

"Some might think I'm dangerous, but with you, my only crime is being dangerously charming."

I nodded, mapping out every part of his beautiful face. Normally, I might roll my eyes at such a cheesy line, but he was definitely guilty.

"Are you okay?" he asked.

How sweet. "Yes, Donte. Now, let's hurry to your place before I change my mind."

The warm Miami air engulfed us as we drove down Collins

Avenue. His car was lithe as a panther cutting through the darkness. The machine zoomed onto the bridge and across Biscayne Bay to the Ritz Carlton, an elegant mix of modern architecture built into a historic cityscape.

We stopped under the front awning, where a valet opened the door for me. Donte was there at once to take my hand and help me out of the low seats. I gazed into his beautiful brown eyes, his magical smile making me melt like butter in a microwave.

He placed his hand on my back and whispered, "You are the most beautiful creature on this planet. You deserve only the best."

I bit my lip, longing with need. A tiny voice in the back of my head faintly called out caution, but that voice was too far away. I wanted him more desperately than I'd ever wanted anyone.

We entered the elevator. When another well-dressed man tried to follow, Donte placed his hand out to stop him from joining us. I could only surmise that he wanted some alone time on the way up to his floor. I watched the stranger disappear between the shutting elevator doors and awaited what would come next.

As the elevator jolted upward, I awaited the feel of Donte's large, firm hands sliding along my hips, but it never happened.

The elevator stopped with a ding, and the doors opened into a vast room with floor-to-ceiling windows framing a fantastic view of downtown Miami. I took it all in, admiring the beauty of the city's profile like a painting or musical score.

Donte's reflection appeared in the glass behind me. I was his for the taking. He placed his hand on my arm and pulled me to face him.

Then he handed me a glass of water and told me to drink.

"Drink all of it. We have all night. I promise you'll thank me later."

I swiftly drank the water, then set the glass on the table next to me. I reached up, placing my hand on his cheek, letting him know I was his for the taking.

He whisked me up into his strong arms, my hand resting on his chest as he carried me to the bedroom. The bedroom was just as large as the living room and claimed another beautiful city view.

He carefully set me on my feet, facing him, as his fingers found the zipper on the back of my dress and gently slid it down my back. Suddenly, I felt weak and a little dizzy.

I stumbled into him as I tried to step out of my dress. I tried to kiss him, but he threw the covers open and set me down on the bed, then gently lifted one foot to remove my shoe. I leaned back on my elbows and tried to watch him, but he kept going out of focus.

No, no, I wanted to remember this. I couldn't be falling asleep.

He removed my other shoe, and then he leaned into me. I wiggled myself to the center of the bed to make room for him to join me.

"Please take me."

That was the last thing I remember saying.

My headache was pounding its way out of my skull.

I was in a strange bed. Instantly, I picked up the covers, relieved to see that I remained somewhat dressed in my bra and panties.

On the nightstand was a travel package of aspirin with a bottle of water, a business card, and a note.

I took the aspirin and read the note:

You are an incredible woman. I would love to meet you again in a more personal setting. I hope the aspirin helps. For reference, Dark adds a little extra euphoria to the drinks of the ladies he wants for his Dark Room. You may want to be careful what you drink next time. I placed you in bed and slept on the sofa. I ordered your dress cleaned and pressed. It should be returned in the morning with your breakfast. I have checked out to return home. Please take your time this morning and use the room as you like before you leave.

Sincerely,

Donte

"I was drugged?" I yelled out into the empty room. Shit! I thought I was just drunk. I couldn't believe I was so careless.

I saw my clutch on the dining table in the other room, stumbled out of bed, and checked to see my gun and badge were still in there. *Whew.*

Sueann's card fell out onto the table. I couldn't believe she and some other women would go into a room like that. Did she know she'd been drugged? I shook my head, disappointed in myself. I might have ended up in that same Dark Room if it weren't for Donte.

Damn. How could I have been so irresponsible? I was drugged

and could have been used like some whore, or worse. Fortunately, Donte was apparently a chivalrous man. Wait, did he drug me too with that glass of water? But then again, he'd never touched me.

I was confused, embarrassed, and angry with myself as I waited for the aspirin to kick in. I should have been leery of the same server bringing drinks directly to us.

How could I have been so stupid?

I hadn't experienced a morning walk of shame since my first frat party in college, when I was drugged. I had vowed to never let that happen again. Yet, here I was.

I jumped at the knock on the door.

"Room service!"

I swiftly put on a bathrobe and answered the door.

"Good morning, ma'am. Mr. Bario asked that we bring you breakfast, these clothes, and this dress this morning."

I felt guilty for not having any gratuity. "Thank you," I said. "You can leave the cart by the table."

Inside the box were a matching hoodie, sweatpants, and tennis shoes that fit me perfectly. How did he know my size?

I went to the bathroom to wash off my makeup and put my hair in a messy bun. Then I slipped into the sweats, stuffed an apple and a container of Yoplait yogurt in my pockets, and called a taxi to meet me in the lobby. I didn't want to stand there holding my dress any longer than necessary. I stared at the business card on the nightstand. It had Donte's information, and on the back, a handwritten phone number—his private number, no doubt.

I was about to throw it in the wastebasket but decided to put it in my clutch. He really was a respectful and delicious-looking man, at least to me, but he also clearly knew more about what happened at Dark's parties. I needed to add him to my list to follow up for questioning.

My car was right where I'd left it in the parking garage of Dark Enterprises. I placed my dress in the back seat and drove home, wondering what kind of drug could have made me feel like that.

When I got home, I soaked myself in the shower, letting the hot water remove the past twelve hours from my body. After I washed my hair, I stared at a random tile on the wall and remembered something I'd forgotten amid my euphoria. My father had worked with the vice president of the United States. What did he do?

Chapter 14

With my Saturday and Sunday off, I recovered with several naps and researched the Hotel Schweizerhof, which had a rich history and was highly esteemed. Then I searched my father's computer, using any keywords to find anything related to him working for the vice president. This blind squirrel hoped to find a nut, but still no luck.

Scelisi should know more. But can I trust him? He did try to protect me last night. I didn't know what to believe.

I went to bed early and went to work refreshed. I wanted to check on my father's record of death. Given the poorly developed reports conducted on the Jane Does, I wasn't going to hold my breath that the examiner report on my father would have more details.

I scrolled through my father's report, desperation setting in. Toxicology had ruled out alcohol, but the results had nothing else. The blood work didn't provide any clues either.

With a heavy heart, I clicked on the folder of photos. My head swam and my eyes blurred at the sight of the mark around his neck—somehow more vivid amid the emptiness of the page. I brushed away my tears and forced myself to look closer, memories flooding back as I examined pictures of his arms and legs for signs of violence, but there were none. The fact that there were no marks on his wrists made murder unlikely, and with no additional neck damage, one could rule out a struggle while he died by the rope. All indicators pointed to suicide, but regardless of the evidence, I refused to believe he would do that to himself, or me.

The medical examiner's report was another dead end. If Dr. Jefferies was involved with my father, she would have to know more. I need to find the truth.

"Good morning, Agent Slade."

Agent Kimmel walked in. I fumbled to close my computer window and stood.

I stood to walk to Kimmel's office and tell her about the folder getting stolen.

"Hey, Slade, have the murder case solved yet?"

Why the hell is Baxter in so early? I laughed inside, seeing him wear the same type of black pants and tweed jacket that Wilson wears, but much cheaper shoes.

"Impressive that you broke away from Wilson's leash, Baxter. There's hope for you yet."

"Ha-ha. I came in early to give Dr. Jefferies a hand with Jane Doe Blonde #2."

Emily, I thought to myself. They were going to get rid of the body, weren't they?

"Why would you be involved in that?" I asked. "That's for the undertaker."

Baxter shook his head smugly. "Ah, Jenna, someday you'll understand how things work around here."

"What does that mean?"

"Baxter!" Wilson bellowed as he walked out of the elevator. "Just do what you're supposed to do."

Baxter walked off toward the elevators. "I'm on it, Agent Wilson."

A subtle tear marred the pocket of Wilson's jacket.

"Can't afford a new jacket?" I asked, pointing.

He looked down and paused. "I must have caught it on something." I discreetly scanned him for more flaws. Then he said, "Agent Slade, I recommend you be careful stepping where you shouldn't. You might just step in some shit you can't get off your shoe."

Instinctively, I looked down at his shoes—and then had an idea.

"Thanks for the advice, Wilson. I'll consider it."

Thirty minutes later, I pulled into the driveway of my house and hurried around the side to the windows overlooking my father's office, searching for any broken branches on a rose bush or a shrub. Even during the day, my FBI-issued flashlight showed every leaf and thorn in sharp relief. If a person had entered through one of these windows, it would be hard to believe they hadn't left behind some broken branch, some imprint in the mulch below.

But I saw nothing suspicious.

It was time to call Smart Tech again.

Back in my father's office, I realized I must have left his computer up and running, as the green light was glowing. I tapped the space bar, and the screen clicked on to reveal picture of some grand building in a browser page.

I definitely hadn't left this there.

I pulled out my gun and went through the house, checking every cabinet, every closet, and every window to ensure they were locked—nothing out of the ordinary.

Then I sat back down in the chair and studied the picture again. The building had large pillars, and the car parked in front seemed to have European plates, but the resolution deteriorated when I zoomed in.

The name on the building was fuzzy as well, but I could make out the word "bank" at the end.

Was this where my father went? Was this in Switzerland?

I googled Swiss banks and found it—the same building.

I was about to look at my calendar to plan a European vacation when Todd arrived.

I guided him to my father's office, explaining, "There are two issues. Someone broke into this window the other night while I was home, and the alarm never sounded. Then today I pulled up my screen to find a photo that definitely wasn't there before. Can you investigate?"

"That would require sophisticated systems and experienced hackers," Todd replied, rubbing his neck. "Does anyone else have access to this computer?"

"I'm the only one here." I wrote the new passwords on a piece of paper and handed it to him. "And Todd . . . there's an extra three hundred dollars in it if you can find out who hacked me."

His eyes sparkled at the offer. "I'll do my best."

As he worked, I couldn't shake the feeling that someone was watching me.

I stared at my murder board while he worked his technical magic. I thought about Kimmel not asking me about the IDs of the Jane Does, and whether I should send her the file.

"Miss Slade!" Todd whispered.

"Yes, Todd?"

He packed up his laptop and wires and gestured for me to follow him. As soon as we walked outside, he said, "I can't be sure, but I think you're being spied on."

"What? How do you know that?"

"There's a backdoor password for your security system that I didn't spot before," he said. "It looks like your security system isn't a stock system."

"What does that mean?"

In a hushed voice, he explained it had an extra back door programmed in so someone could manipulate it.

"Who could do such a thing?" I asked quietly.

"The only organization I can think of is the federal government," he said soberly. "Ma'am, I think it's best if you find someone else. Something strange is happening here. I've seen this stuff in too many movies, and I don't want to be in the news next week."

With that, he headed for his car and drove away without getting paid.

I shut the door behind him and shouted, "What in the hell is happening?" Silence filled the house again when the echo dissipated. Had the FBI done this when they swept through my dad's things? Was Scelisi behind this?

I should have asked Todd to check the desktop computer first. I wanted to know how a photo of a bank had ended up on the computer.

Maybe my father had uncovered something, and it was stashed in this bank. What was Scelisi after, and why did my dad hide it? Was he involved with the vice president, or some bad actor?

The pieces spun in my mind. A trip to Switzerland seemed like an obvious decision, but could it be a trap? So, I had the key, only to have whatever was in the vault stolen from me?

I needed to be prepared for anything.

Chapter 15

The bright morning sun shone through the windows as the plane descended toward the city of Bern, and yet my inner conflict was driving me nuts. Part of me was hopeful that I would learn more, but another part was apprehensive.

Kimmel had questioned my request to go on a quick European vacation while in the middle of a case, but when I told her I might have a lead on the key, she approved my travel. Unfortunately, I didn't have time to get diplomatic clearance to carry my service weapon.

I took a taxi to the Hotel Schweizerhof.

"Hello, my name is Jenna Slade, and I have a reservation here for a few days?"

"Was your journey a pleasant one, Miss Slade?" she inquired gracefully as she checked my documents. Her splendid blue eyes were captivating, brilliant cobalt gems—she was truly beautiful.

"Yes, it was, thank you."

"One moment, please." She smiled before walking away.

I glanced around the lobby, in awe of its magnificence. Huge paintings of castles in the mountains hung from golden frames, and statues of women in different poses abounded. One portrayed a woman pouring water from an urn.

An older, clean-shaven, balding man in a handsome wool suit appeared at the counter along with the clerk. He scanned me and my suitcase, looked at the computer screen, my passport, and then back at me.

"Welcome, Miss Slade. I am Sergio, the hotel manager here."

"Thank you for the warm welcome. Is everything all right?"

"Yes, but we will need additional identification, Miss Slade. Would you please follow me?"

Sergio opened a waist-high door nearby, inviting me to go through it. As I didn't have my service weapon, I felt quite vulnerable.

The clerk smiled reassuringly.

Sergio led me into a well-lit room with a couple of chairs, a table, and a computer. Connected to it were some instruments that included a retina scanner.

"Would you please look into this hole on this retina scanner and focus on the green light?"

A retina scan for a hotel room?

"I don't understand. Why do I need—"

130

"Please, miss, it will all be clear when we positively identify you."

I looked into the hole and saw the little green light in the middle of the darkness. It was a typical system, but I was skeptical, as it would require my retina map to match. How would they have that?

"Okay, miss, will you place your right index finger in this little hole? You will feel a pinprick."

Bewildered, I placed my finger in the device on the counter that looked like a small black mousetrap.

The man looked at a monitor and smiled. "Okay, Miss Slade, we've positively identified you."

"I could have told you that. What's this all about?"

"We were instructed that, if you were to check in, we should positively identify you before we provided you access to the vault."

"Vault? What vault? I just wanted a room."

"Yes, miss, we will give you your room, but if you have your key, I will take you to your secure box."

I froze. How did he know about the key? Wasn't it to a security box at the bank? The key was secure in my makeup kit . . . which was left in the lobby.

"I left it in the lobby!"

My lungs took in a sudden rush of air. Was this a distraction to get the key?

The clerk had brought my bags inside the small door. *Whew.* I took a deep breath to reduce my heart rate.

"Is everything all right, Miss Slade?" the desk clerk asked.

The manager cleared his throat. "Miss, are you ready?"

"Yes, Sergio, thank you, just a moment."

I couldn't help but think my father coordinated all of this before he died, but why? How would he know I'd be here? After checking to make sure no one else was around, I reached into the front pocket of my sizable purple suitcase, pulled out my makeup kit, opened an empty bottle of makeup remover, and poured the key into my hand.

The manager smiled at the sight of it. "Right this way, miss."

I followed him down a hallway to small elevator, narrow enough that it could fit no more than four people.

"Miss, please place your key in this slot, if you will." He pointed to what appeared to be a small slit above the floor numbers. There were no other markings. He placed another key in an adjacent hole. It likely required two keys to get to the secure floor.

I placed the key inside, and the doors closed.

I was surprised by our descent. When we finally stopped, the doors opened to a small hub, which branched off to five dimly lit hallways.

"Where are we?" I asked Sergio.

"We're in our secure vault. This is the most secure vault in the world . . . but then, I am biased."

"How do I know which hallway to go down?"

"You have a green key. If you look at the entrance to each hallway, they are color coded. The green one is this way." He gestured to the second hallway from the right.

"How do you know this is a green key?"

"You'll see the letter G below the handle, miss."

We walked to the green hallway, and as we approached, lights clicked on above, showing a long corridor with what looked like over a hundred doors on either side.

"How do I know which door goes to this key?"

"That is an excellent question, miss. Your key is a proximity card. When you're near the correct door, the door lock will illuminate. It's another security feature."

I nodded as we began our trek, feeling like I was in a scene right out of *Alice in Wonderland*. My heart was racing. I couldn't help but think I was in a trap and I'd never see daylight again.

Suddenly, Sergio stopped and gestured to the glowing door lock. "It would appear this is your door, miss. If you like, I can stay here with you, or I can wait at the end of the hallway."

My father had gone to great lengths to coordinate all of this before he died. What if this manager was part of the organization that wanted whatever is inside that door? "It's best if I'm alone. Thank you."

"As you wish, miss."

When he was far enough away, I studied the green glow emanating from beneath the lock, and spotted a small slot just like the one on the elevator. My hand shook as I slipped the key into the hole and turned it.

A click sounded, and I was in.

My eyes widened. Numerous identical black briefcases filled the shelves, piled three high. I counted around forty—each with its own lock, the key already in it.

The closest case contained neatly bundled stacks of US hundred-dollar bills, similar to what one might see at a bank or in a CIA movie. Another had stacks of euros. Each one I opened contained more cash and nothing else. I opened and opened until only one case remained, sitting on the shelf by itself.

Whatever my father was involved in, it must have been substantial, because there were millions of dollars in this room.

When I opened the last one, all that remained was another key in a foam slot.

Was this what Scelisi wanted? And how had my father known I would come here?

I turned in a circle, trying to comprehend the enormity of what I'd just uncovered.

I grabbed the new key, placed it in my jacket pocket, and closed the briefcase. At the door, I took one last look at this strange room, wondering why my father had hidden millions of dollars in this vault on the other side of the world.

"I hope everything is up to your expectations, miss?" Sergio said when I met him back in the hub.

"Yes, it looks great." I fished out my new key. "Is this a key to another vault?"

"No, miss, that key belongs to the National Bank. It's about a kilometer away. Do you need directions?"

"That would be helpful, thank you." So, the key from that little piggy bank didn't go to the bank, but this new key I found in the briefcase did. "Did you know my father?" I suddenly inquired as we began our ascent back to the lobby.

"We have many guests who like our secure environment. We don't ask questions, nor do we remember any names, so I can't recall anyone in particular. I hope you understand."

I nodded as we continued to ascend. My mind was a tornado of thoughts on what my father could have been involved in, how he came into all this cash, and what was in that other vault that couldn't be here in this one? Was the cash mine to take?

The elevator doors opened.

Stepping out, Sergio gave me his polite farewell. "If there will be nothing else, you may proceed to the front desk, where Celia will set you up with your room. She can also provide you directions to the bank."

"Thank you very much," I said.

"My pleasure, miss," he answered with a smile. I returned one of my own and gave a small wave before continuing to the front desk, where beautiful Celia awaited.

"Hello, Celia! Sergio said you could help me get settled in my room."

"Yes! Everything's all ready for you. We've even taken your luggage there already. Your card has your room number written on it, and the whole stay is prepaid. The elevator's across the lobby if you need it. Also, any services you require are available here . . . any service!"

"Who prepaid for my room?"

"It was a Mr. Charles Slade."

"My father?" My question was more of a surprised gasp. "When did he prepay for this room?"

"Let me see." She stared at her screen. "It appears he paid for it today."

"That's impossible. My father died nearly nine years ago."

"That's what I have in my notes, miss."

There was no way.

"*How* did he pay for it?"

"It appears he paid in credit. He does have a significant amount of credit with our hotel."

I couldn't believe what I was hearing. "How much credit?"

"He has approximately 400,000 euros in credit, Miss. You are authorized to use it for whatever you need."

"Surely you have some way to confirm his identity to prevent someone from using his credit," I said, still struggling to contain my shock. Part of me wants to believe he's alive, but why now? Why after all these years? I just saw the pictures showing him dead— didn't I?

"Yes, ma'am. He has a six-digit confirmation, which we link to his phone number on file, and upon his confirmation to the code, we accept it is him. And now with your identification confirmation, we will link you to the same account per our instructions on file."

"But, in theory, it could be anyone who has access to his old phone number and that six-digit passcode." Could Scelisi have coordinated my coming here in order to get the keys—or where they lead?

"In theory, yes, but that would be for the client to safeguard."

"May I have directions to the National Bank?"

"Yes, of course, but the bank is closed today. It will be open tomorrow morning." She pulled out a map of the city, circled a small picture of the hotel, and then drew a course to where the bank was located.

"Thank you very much."

Shifting my gaze across the lobby, a wave of strange emotions ran through my body—suspicion, anxiety, and familiarity all at once. A woman cuddled her rat-like dog while a suited man walked past and a couple checked in at the counter. Was somebody watching me, or following me? I thought to myself that between now and tomorrow morning was a lot of time to coordinate an ambush on me. I'd need to be vigilant with every step I made.

It was only in the elevator that I realized the key envelope read "Penthouse." When the doors opened, I was met with a mansion rather than a hallway.

Luxurious furniture, sparkling chandeliers, fresh flowers in vases, and exotic paintings adorned the walls. This room put Donte's penthouse to shame.

I pulled out the map to see if I was lucky enough to see my path to the bank through my window, but no such luck. Still, the beautiful buildings and fountains were majestic, almost like art themselves.

My eyes finally came to rest on a decanter of brown liquid just next to a large window overlooking most of Bern. Instinctively, I poured some into a glass and took a sip—it was my father's favorite scotch.

Confusion boiled within me. Who was my father, and how did I end up here? Was he guiding me? Or was someone else?

Chapter 16

The next morning, a knock startled me from a peaceful sleep.

Throwing on my robe, I peered through the peephole. A young man in a crisp hotel uniform stood outside.

"Who is it?" I called out cautiously.

"It's room service, ma'am," he said with a distinctly American accent. "Complimentary for the penthouse suite."

I grabbed a small bronze statue from the table and held it behind my back as I opened the door. The attendant wheeled in an ornate cart covered with fine linen and several chrome-lidded serving dishes.

"Stop for a moment," I commanded as I pulled off the platter covers one by one, inspecting each plate, only to find nothing but freshly prepared breakfast food.

"Is everything all right, ma'am?" the server asked politely, his brow furrowed.

"Why do you use the term 'ma'am'? You must be American. What state?"

"I'm from Georgia but came here for college to study advanced cybersecurity."

"How did you end up in Switzerland?"

He explained as he set the dining table. "It was luck, really. I saw this ad to apply for a scholarship, which everyone said was a scam, but no one could believe it was real when I won it."

He listed off all the items he'd brought: scrambled eggs with cheese and condiments, sausage links, potatoes, waffles, and a bowl of fresh fruit.

I slowly replaced the statue on the entry table, hoping he didn't notice.

"Will there be anything else, ma'am?"

The breakfast looked fabulous. I walked to my coat pocket, pulled out my wallet, and handed him ten euros. "That will be good. Thank you . . ."

"Justin, ma'am."

"Thank you, Justin. Will you be the only one providing room service to this room?"

"During the day, ma'am. At night, I believe it will be Cali. She's about the same age as me, but she's from Sweden."

"Thank you, Justin."

My stomach groaned at the smell of the food as soon as he left.

My body was about six hours ahead, and I'd had a light dinner—I was suddenly starving.

It was one of the best breakfasts I'd ever had. I savored my morning meal while looking out upon the capital of Switzerland, trying to solve a puzzle where pieces were piling up, but nothing seemed to connect.

I had an hour to kill before the bank opened, so a tour of the city seemed like the right thing to do—it would be a good way to see if someone was following me. I'd rather know early versus getting trapped somewhere later.

As I walked through the streets with two invaluable keys in my pocket, I couldn't stop the hopeful thoughts that perhaps my late father was alive. Did he walk these streets? I would have loved to stroll through the city with him. I'd look in every direction, every corner, every alleyway entrance in hopes he might be alive and watching me right now, but he was never there.

I strolled around and took in the beauty of the city. Everywhere I looked was stunning. I couldn't believe this city existed long before America. As I looked at the marvelous sites, I made sure to glance around me to see whether I recognized any faces or saw anyone lurking. This was a technique we'd learned for stakeouts that some just don't get the hang of and try to overact the part. Reading a newspaper against a streetlight or on a park bench was too obvious, shopping in a store was a little more convincing.

The path eventually led me beneath a stunning clock tower and past vendors selling sweet treats and hot food, from bratwurst to warm soft pretzels and a lot of chocolate. My eyes circled suspiciously. Was the man on the park bench really just reading? Was the woman grabbing croissants just hungry?

My steps soon led me over an old stone bridge crossing the Aare River that flowed through Bern. I stopped at its midpoint and admired the view, longing for a real vacation. The bridge connected to a monument built by the Dukes of Zähringen in 1191. It made me wonder—how had they even gone about creating this city?

When I finally made it to the bank, a young man greeted me in a foreign language.

"Hello, do you speak English?"

"Of course, miss. My name is Farley. What can I do for you?"

"My father left me this key, and I'm told it opens something in this bank?" I showed him the key I'd found in the last briefcase at the hotel vault.

"What is your name, miss?"

"Jenna Slade."

His brief look of surprise instantly changed to a smile. Grabbing a phone, he said something in a foreign language that sounded like German, but I couldn't understand it. He hung up.

"Please follow me, Miss Slade."

We went beyond the lobby, where he used an access card to open a heavy steel door. Then he led me into a room full of lockboxes that ranged in size from that of a post office box to something that could fit a human inside.

"Please wait here a moment, Miss Slade."

142

He walked through another door as I gazed at the vast number of small gray boxes.

When he reappeared, he was accompanied by an older man with a bald head, and a long gray beard and mustache. His hunched back and slow movements were unsettling, and his voice was strained, as though he'd been smoking his entire life. "Miss Slade, will you follow me?"

He led me to an office, where he sluggishly walked around his desk, steadying himself on its edge with his hand.

"Miss Slade. You have a key for our bank?"

After taking it from me and placing it in a slot at the top of a small black box, he sat down behind his computer.

"Who is Charles Slade?" he asked.

"He's my father and left this key for me."

"Your father has rented the most secure vault we offer, Miss Slade, so please forgive us for our due diligence."

"Of course," I replied. After all, having already had a retina scan and DNA check, what was one more hoop?

"Will you please place your finger in this little box?" he asked.

I reluctantly did so. The little pinprick was the same, but so subtle that there was no blood. A million thoughts about what my father could have been involved in raced through my mind—and none of them were good.

"Thank you, Miss Slade. I've confirmed you're related to Mr. Charles Slade, and I have a note here that, upon proof of DNA, will take you to the vault. Will you follow me?"

He gave the key back to me, placed his keycard near the door next to him, and walked through. I followed him, while Farley remained behind.

We walked down a long hallway with doors on each side about every ten feet.

"This is your room," the man said, stopping in front of me. Not paying attention, I bumped into his arm.

"Sorry."

"It's perfectly fine, Miss Slade. I'll be in my office if you require assistance."

I watched him slowly return to his office, then looked at the door. There was no green glow like the previous vault. I placed my key in the little slot and heard a metallic click.

As the room illuminated with recessed lighting, my heart sank— another black briefcase, but this time, only one.

Inside was an external hard drive no bigger than my hand.

What the hell was on this hard drive to warrant all this protection? You would think the Vatican's secrets were on this thing. Was this what Scelisi was trying to get, or was he after all that money in the other vault?

I leaned against the wall and contemplated everything that had happened in the past week. Scelisi wouldn't have been able to get in without passing the DNA test, not without a lot of preparation. Was he the one leading me here? Or was it my father himself?

I looked down at the tiny device in my palm. The hard drive looked like any other one that plugged into a USB port. If I plugged it into my bureau laptop, it would surely get flagged right away. I could leave it here until I sorted out more, but if the contents of this drive were so important for someone to lead me here, it was important to take. Still, I had to find some way to access this information, and before I became a target.

Unless I had been a target all along.

Tucking the hard drive in my jacket pocket, I marched out with the now-empty briefcase as a decoy.

"I'm finished," I told the older gentleman. "Thank you for protecting this so well."

"My pleasure, Miss Slade. Farley will take you back outside."

I followed Farley back into the massive room of small lockboxes. But just when we were about to go through the heavy steel door, he whipped around, a gun in his hand.

"I'll be taking that briefcase, Miss Slade."

The nearest exit was another fifty feet in front of me, while the secure place I'd just left was about the same distance behind me. I had put the drive in my coat pocket expecting the briefcase to potentially get grabbed, but I didn't expect it to happen here in the bank, or at gunpoint.

My stomach sank like a rock, causing me to step back, only to bump into a giant of a man holding another gun to my back. His gigantic figure loomed over me.

"Very powerful people want that briefcase, so you can hand it over willingly, or we can kill you here and take it by force," he said, his voice low. "I'd much prefer not to make a mess."

My mind instantly returned to the academy training, trying to remember which move would help me escape this situation. Each one involved my service weapon, which I didn't have. I needed to get creative.

"How did you know I'd come here?"

Farley replied, "We didn't, which is why I've been working in this god-awful bank full of elitists for the last seven years, waiting for this very day. Once you checked into your hotel, we were prepared for you to show up. Now, hand over the briefcase and you can continue with your dull American life."

I dropped the briefcase in front of him. Keeping his gun trained on me, he picked it up. Acting on instinct, I spun around, gripping the man behind me by his hand, and kicked Farley in the face. He flew backward with the sound of a gunshot as he fired toward the ceiling. The larger man grabbed my hand and pulled away, but not before I twisted his gun out of his hand and shot at Farley.

He fell backward as his bodyguard launched himself on top of me, gripping me so tight I thought he would crush my ribs. Desperate for air and with limited movement, I angled his gun toward what I believed was his leg and rapidly fired three rounds.

He released me, screaming in pain, and fell to the floor, holding his leg.

Farley took a shot at me—he missed, but I didn't. I hit him twice

146

in the chest. He fell to the floor and blood pooled around him. He had to be dead.

An ear-splitting dissonance of sirens and alarms ripped through the corridor as officers came barreling in, guns drawn. Fierce, foreign commands hurtled from their lips. I dropped the gun and raised my hands above my head, shaking with fear as the police formed a tight half-circle around me. One inched closer until he could roughly grab my arm and cuff my hands behind my back.

The cold muzzle of a gun against the nape of my neck shattered my efforts to remain calm.

"I am an FBI agent from America!" I frantically shouted as they led me out of the bank. "Does anyone speak English? That is my briefcase they tried to steal from me."

The officers paid me no heed, banging my head into the entrance to the police car before shoving me into the back seat. The door slammed with a deafening clang, and then all was silent except for my briefcase being tossed onto the seat beside me.

I would have failed this exercise at the Academy for not being gentle enough to someone under arrest.

The interrogation room was identical to ours back home, but it smelled different. The damp, musty odor made me uneasy. I'd hate to go through this and end up sick from some Swiss mold spores.

They'd taken my wallet, badge, and the hard drive from my jacket. Now they were all laid out on the table I was cuffed to. The bindings on my wrists were already digging into my skin.

Farley was the first person I'd ever killed. I hadn't gotten to choose whether I pulled the trigger; it just happened. My instincts from training paid off. Both of them had been threats to me, and I did what was necessary. I only hoped the Swiss police would see it that way.

It was a waiting game at this point. A game I'd sat in on many times.

The door swung open, revealing an older man in a pristine blue-and-white pinstriped suit. He was clean-shaven except for a small goatee.

"Good afternoon, Miss Slade. I am Chief Inspector Sergento."

"Good morning, Chief Inspector. The name is Agent Slade."

He looked down briefly to read something in his folder. "Apologies, Agent Slade." He reached into his pocket and produced a key. "Let me take these off you. We needed to ensure that you were, indeed, who you claimed. Your special agent in charge— Kimmel—informed us that you came here to investigate a murder in America. You should have contacted us when you arrived so we could best assist you and prevent such a situation from happening."

I was shocked that Kimmel backed me, but I wasn't looking forward to explaining myself when I returned home.

After the inspector removed the handcuffs, I rubbed my sore wrists. Even though I had role-played as the bad guy before, I had never worn handcuffs for this long.

The inspector sat down across from me and opened the briefcase from the vault. I had never reset the lock after I removed the hard drive.

"Why would a bank lobby assistant risk his life and kill you for an empty briefcase?" he asked curiously. "By the way, he died. The other gentleman you shot will live, but he, too, will be questioned."

I shrugged, but my heart was pounding in my chest. I had mixed feelings about killing Farley, but I had to keep my focus on getting out of there.

"Perhaps he thought this"—the inspector picked up the hard drive in question—"was inside?"

"That's definitely one possibility," I replied. "But how would this armed bank employee know who I was? Much less have another large, armed accomplice waiting inside the secure safe-deposit box room to steal my briefcase? It's all quite strange, if you ask me."

"Yes, those are all good questions," the inspector agreed. "The man who was injured is a security guard for powerful people. He will likely be released after his injury heals. I trust you won't be staying in Switzerland much longer?"

"I was hoping to do some sightseeing, but I suspect it's best I return home soon."

"There is a flight leaving for Miami in three hours. I think it's important for you to be on that flight, Agent Slade. I don't know who else might be looking for . . . that briefcase." He touched the hard drive again. "You are free to take your belongings and go. A patrol car will take you to your hotel."

I placed my badge and hard drive in my jacket and picked up the briefcase. "Thank you, Chief Inspector. I'll do what I can to be on that plane."

"Agent Slade," he said when I reached the door. "These are bad, influential people. I wish you good luck."

Back at the hotel, I packed quickly. When I got to my laptop, I paused. Plugging in my external hard drive wasn't worth the risk, but I desperately wanted to know what was on this thing someone would have killed me over.

Justin!

Justin answered the line. "Good evening, Miss Slade. How can I help you?"

"Do you have a personal laptop at work?"

"Um, ma'am, I do, but . . ."

"Can you bring it up here? I need some IT expertise, and I'll make it worth your while."

"Yes, ma'am, I'll be right up."

As soon as Justin arrived, wearing a backpack, I pulled the hard drive out of my jacket pocket.

"Can you see what's on this hard drive for me? I'll get in trouble if my job detects anything plugged into my work laptop." It wasn't quite a lie.

"Um, do you know what's on here? I'd hate to get a virus and mess up my laptop."

"I'll give you a hundred euros to try. If it messes up your laptop, I'll get you the newest model."

"Okay."

His laptop fired right up.

"Wow, that was fast," I mentioned.

"It's the highest-end solid state with—"

"I got it, outstanding laptop. Sorry for cutting you short, but I have to catch a flight and want to know what's on this thing before I leave."

He took the hard drive and plugged it into his USB port. A small screen popped up, asking for a password.

Justin looked up at me. "Do you know the password?"

If it was my father coordinating this, I would think he would use a password I would know, but nothing came to mind. I just shook my head.

"Let me take a crack at it," he said and opened an app on his computer.

A scanning screen came up, and we watched the animation of a scan bar getting filled in. Then it stopped with a note stating 264-bit encryption.

He looked up to me. "Yeah, unless you know what this is, there's no way I can help. That's much too big of a passcode for me to try."

I stared at the words on the screen and nodded. "Thanks, Justin. I appreciate you trying."

I pulled a hundred euros from my wallet and handed it to him after he packed up his laptop. "Good luck with your schooling here."

"Thanks, Ms. Slade. Have a safe flight back to the States."

Chapter 17

As I stepped off the plane, someone suddenly bumped into me, and my heart skipped a beat. Agent Kimmel was next to me with tight lips.

"Agent Kimmel, I didn't know—"

"There are many things you don't know, Jenna. Now get out of their way and come over here," she commanded, looking at the passengers backed up behind me.

Kimmel meeting me at the airport could not be good. Although she approved my going to Switzerland, she probably wasn't expecting me to shoot a couple of people, and kill one. She could decide my fate right then and there—she wasn't even going to have me come into the office to collect my badge and gun.

"I risked my job vouching for you in Switzerland. I've already received a call from the State Department and my boss today. Now I need to know what the hell you found out there, and don't give me any tap-dancing bullshit."

She ushered me into a security room, where we found a small area to sit down and talk.

"Okay, spill the beans. I want to know everything about that key," she said.

I paused for a moment, wondering if I should take the risk. Ultimately, I decided to tell her everything Scelisi had said, my suspicions about my security system, and the second key I'd discovered in the hotel vault. I didn't think she needed to know about the cash or my suspicions of my father being alive. At least not yet.

"Jenna. Your father worked directly for me, and he worked undercover. He had infiltrated Dark Enterprises' networks and was compiling evidence that implicated extremely influential elitists worldwide. These powerful people paid him handsomely, but his ethics didn't allow him to keep the money. His death surprised me, but once again, we are dealing with very *powerful people*. I believe the only reason you're still alive is because they need you to bring them what they're looking for, and it may be on that hard drive. We must understand what's on it. I'm under surveillance, which is why I left you to do much of the legwork. I need you, Jenna. I hope you can trust me."

I looked down at the floor. "Can I speak frankly?"

"Of course."

"You know Wilson has been falsifying records of the Jane Does. In all probability, you also know he has been blackmailing Dr. Jefferies to falsify autopsy reports, yet you've done nothing. When I told you I lost the photos, you weren't concerned. How am I to trust you when I don't know where you stand?"

She nodded, clearly deliberating over her response. "I understand your perspective and appreciate it. There are many moving parts well beyond what we see on the surface, and I don't have the freedom I once had." She pursed her lips, as if she were fighting back sad emotions. "Your father was a very good man, and I had to disavow him when he died, or I may have met the same fate. Senior leadership doesn't think much of a younger agent sticking her nose in places she shouldn't. But it seems as if Scelisi may know more than I thought."

"If someone killed my father, Dr. Jefferies would know the truth!" I whispered, still unsure if he was dead or alive.

"Jenna, I ask that you don't ask her just yet. She is fragile right now, and I'd hate for her to meet the same fate. She knows too much, but they still need her . . . for now."

"Why not just arrest Wilson and waterboard his ass?"

She flashed me a wry smile. "I would like nothing more, but there are senior leaders who would have him released in no time."

"Then what's your plan?" I asked.

"I have an ally in senior leadership who is waiting for enough proof to launch a mass arrest—but we need it to be absolute. If there's anything that won't hold up in court, we can kiss our careers goodbye."

I nodded, understanding her unspoken warning: Kissing our careers goodbye might be the least of our concerns.

"Jenna, tell me you still have a copy of the photos and the names associated with them."

"Yes," I said. "I have a soft copy of them. Fortunately, I scanned them before Scelisi showed up," I said.

"You're brilliant, Jenna. Just make sure you store them somewhere safe."

I inhaled a sense of pride. So much had happened in a short period of time, it was nice to get a pat on the back.

"Don't trust anyone, Jenna." Silence filled the room for a moment. "Come. I'll walk you to your car."

The sinister Dodge Charger was parked in front of my neighbor's house, but it didn't have Scelisi's license plates. I was relieved and yet alarmed. My stomach clenched defensively as I pulled up beside it. The tinted windows were opaque, like dark eyes observing me from within.

I crept out of my car and cautiously approached. The door was locked, and nothing stirred but a chill wind that whistled through the trees. I slowly walked to the house, scanning all around to watch for anyone moving.

My alarm chirped when I entered. I keyed in the code and pulled out my gun, ready to confront whatever evil lurked inside. But after searching through each room, I let out a relieved, yet disappointed, breath. The only thing out of place was the rancid smell emanating from the fridge, which told me just how out of control my Chinese takeout problem had gotten.

I walked out to my back porch and peered between the two houses—the sinister black car was gone, leaving nothing but an eerie sense that someone had been waiting to confirm my return. I walked to my car and drove it home.

Back inside, I placed the drive with my other mystery prizes in the safest place I knew.

At my father's desk, I searched through the drawers, pulling them out and looking them over for some set of words or numbers or anything that gave an appearance of a password or, perhaps, a portion of one. He would have hidden them in the house.

I slammed the top drawer shut, perhaps a little harder than intended.

"Damn it, Dad! What the hell are you doing to me?" I yelled out.

I pulled out all the drawers in the tables and cabinets also, but I didn't find anything.

My burner phone rang. At this point, it was 1:00 a.m. Only two people knew this phone number, and D was not the one calling me.

"Hamilton?" I answered.

"Hey, Slade, sorry if I woke you, but you're going to owe me big-time for—"

"Wait! I need to go somewhere else."

If my house was bugged, I didn't want anyone to hear what he had to say. Just answering with his name was probably an oversight.

I walked outside and into my car.

"Okay, Hamilton. I can talk now."

"You won't believe what I stumbled on. Where did you get these files?"

"I can't say."

"Well, I didn't have time to track all the offshore account numbers, but the few I did, I was able to trace to some influential people. Whenever the trust funds reached nearly 100 to 120 million, they were zeroed out and distributed in multiple directions. And you'd never guess where one distribution goes?"

"The vice president?"

"How'd you know? Actually, it was to his son. Once I saw that, I stopped tracing. Jenna, this is the type of information you find right before people go missing and are never found."

"Just a minute. I'll be right back."

I placed the phone on mute and ran back into the house, picked up the Jane Doe case folders, and ran back to the car.

"When did the trust fund closeouts occur?" I asked.

"Many trusts have been closed out over the past twenty years. One of them was May 19, 2015." I didn't have anything there. "Next one was August 3, 2018."

Jane Doe Blonde had died on July 25, 2018.

I looked at the file for Jane Doe Brunette. "Was there another closeout dated around January 5, 2020?"

"Yeah, how did you know? Zahra Trust Fund was zeroed out on the fifteenth."

The only thing I could think of was . . . *wow!* All my training and knowledge, and the only word that came to mind upon uncovering a massive operation that involved sex and murder, was *wow.* The thought of being told Emily had taken her trust fund and moved to Greece, and her body popped up. They're using these women, and when they're killed, they distribute the trust fund to the beneficiaries. Sueann would be next.

"Slade, you still there?"

"Yeah. Can you trace where all those funds went to after the trusts were closed out?"

Hamilton replied, "Yeah, it's all in the document I have, but it's too vast to list over the phone. Oh, and even more important . . ."

More important than connecting the dots to murder cases and money laundering? "What?"

"Those building supplies listed in the document? Nuts, bolts, screws . . ."

"Yeah?"

"I did some cross-agency analysis, and it happens to be the same quantity of different arms and bullets going to the same country. They aren't shipping building supplies. Whoever is doing this is shipping arms masked as building supplies to slip through customs."

Was that what Wilson and Baxter were up to? What about my father? What was he going to do with all that money? Was he going to turn it in once all the guilty are indicted, but since he died, it was stuck in the vault? Is that why Scelisi wanted the key?

"Jenna?"

"Yeah, thanks, Hamilton. Can you send what you have back to me via FedEx? I can't trust any electronic messaging."

"Sure thing, Slade. I'll get to FedEx this afternoon and mail it overnight."

"Thanks, Hamilton, and if all goes well, I may just take a vacation to Germany after this case is closed."

"I'll keep you to that!" He laughed. "Go back to sleep. Let me know when you get it."

"I will, and again, thanks!"

It was good to catch up with him after all these years. The Bureau must have done well for him, as he was full of enthusiasm compared to when I remember him last. I do remember him being quite handsome. I just hope I don't set him up for trouble.

Chapter 18

Waking up was not easy, if I could even call it waking up. I don't think there had been much sleep at all with all my tossing and turning throughout the night. I was haunted by the continuing sense that someone was watching me. Even the faint green light on the smoke detector was suspect. My instincts screamed at me to leave the house and stay anywhere else, but since I've found clues in the house and have yet to find the passcode, I have to stay here, albeit with a higher sense of caution.

My mind raced, trying to understand what the password could be for that hard drive. Two hundred and sixty-four characters could be anything.

I placed all of my evidence on the kitchen table as I ate expired blueberry yogurt—the only food left in my fridge that hadn't gone bad, or at least didn't smell bad.

There were two digital keys for Swiss vaults, and a hard drive that had cost a lot of effort, and nearly my life, to retrieve. I had also obtained Jane Doe photographs on a thumb drive, and case files with purposely omitted information. Soon, I'd have enough evidence from Hamilton to put many prominent people worldwide in jail.

I poured myself a strong cup of coffee and took all the evidence to my father's office, where I set all the pieces on the table with the bourbon and wrote sticky notes. I placed the pins he used for the pictures and strung the red yarn between clues again. I'd take it down again in case someone did break in, but I needed someplace where I could think.

I settled in to figure out what these items meant together, turning a puzzle of a few names into a robust murder board that even my academy professor would be proud of.

I had my suspicions, but soon, it became alarmingly apparent. All the string intersections had two common connections: Dark Enterprises and the FBI.

I need Hamilton to come here and confirm this shit.

I couldn't let anyone see what I put together on the wall. I took a picture with my phone, removed everything from the corkboard, and hid everything in the same secure place. Then I needed to get to work.

Chapter 19

The office was abuzz. Prime ministers from overseas were arriving, and the national security associate assistant director was present. Something big was happening—but thankfully, I wasn't involved.

When my screen turned on, I spotted an email from Hamilton, sent late last night, despite my warning not to contact me electronically:

Call me ASAP.

It was early afternoon in Europe, so I sent Hamilton a text on my burner: *Did you email me on company email?*

The rest of my inbox only had a few irrelevant emails regarding company policy, so I deleted them.

Kimmel's office was dark, with the door closed, and Wilson was nowhere around. I took a walk to the basement and checked on Dr. Jefferies. Kimmel had advised me not to, but I couldn't help myself.

The stainless-steel exam tables looked clean enough to eat off.

There was no sign of Dr. Jefferies or any bodies.

Her office door was locked. Looking through the window, I saw file cabinets, a desk with a computer, and a table with many different medical and forensics textbooks. To my surprise, there were also mysteries by Cornwell, Clancy, Patterson, Grisham, and Agatha Christie.

I walked to the coolers, where the bodies would be stored, and opened one, hoping to find the latest Jane Doe found in the dumpster so I could determine whether an actual autopsy was done. But it was empty, and there was nothing but cold air, like opening my freezer door.

I gently closed that one and opened another. Again, empty. I was about to open a third when—

"Can I help you?"

Dr. Jefferies was behind me, wearing her white coat, with her hands on her hips.

"Um, yeah, I wanted to see what happened to the Jane Doe who was here the other day."

"Since there was no positive identification, she was cremated."

"Did you record her DNA by chance, in case someone queried about her?"

"I gave my report to Agent Wilson." Her gaze dropped to the floor. "I'm sorry, I can't help you."

Many variations of how to ask about my father ran through my head, but none of them presented themselves. Still, after what I overheard with Wilson, I knew she was in a difficult position.

"I can help you," I said.

Her eyes darted to mine, and then looked down again. "You can't help me, and it's best that you don't get involved." She gestured toward the exit. "You'd better leave now."

I walked toward the hallway leading to the elevator and turned to see her hovering by her office door. "There was more to my father's death, wasn't there? I need to know if he's out there."

"Good day, Agent Slade," she said, but then, there—a small nod.

My eyes lit up. She was being monitored, but had given me what I wanted to know. I mouthed a thank-you, but what did she actually tell me?

I'd come back to Dr. Becky Jefferies later.

I looked at my phone for a reply from Hamilton—nothing.

It was time to do some questioning at Dark Enterprises.

Chapter 20

When I checked into the lobby at Dark Enterprises and showed my badge, the receptionist surprised me by pulling out a green badge of her own.

"Oh yes, Agent Slade. We have a badge for you right here." She placed it on a card reader that lit up with a yellow light, and then pointed to a numeric keypad. When Trevor said he'd give me access, I didn't expect my own access card. I followed her instructions to get a passcode, and the light color changed to green.

"You're all set, Agent Slade. This card provides access to all rooms you've been cleared to enter."

"Mr. Dark said I'd have complete access," I fibbed, wanting to see if she'd drop any insight into what rooms I *didn't* have access to.

"You do, Agent Slade, but some areas are highly secure and would require an escort."

"Which rooms are those?"

"That is information you'll need to get from Mr. Dark."

I smiled and nodded. "Thank you very much."

Okay, where to start? I was curious why Dark Enterprises started on the fifth floor of the building, however, everything in the lobby was associated with the company. Walking to the information plaque by the elevators, I saw three different companies on floors two, three, and four: Sahara Security Services, Xi Strategic Consulting, and Paramount Certified Public Accounting.

I pressed the number five in the elevator and began my ascent, focusing on what I was here to do rather than the beautiful Indian theme. Dark Enterprises was in the middle of everything I'd uncovered so far. It was time to shake the tree and see if I could get a few more nuts to fall.

I stepped out into the tiled business hallway with burnt-orange wallpaper. I placed my access card against the security panel across the way, and the green light came on.

Click.

Success.

Inside, the fluorescent lights flickered, casting an unflattering glow on the gray cubicles. Some employees were busy working away on their computers, while others chatted about their weekend plans. I pretended to be lost, wandering around to get a glimpse of what was going on in this mysterious office. I drifted toward the windows with a view of the alleyway where the body had been found. Three cubicles overlooked the crime scene.

I approached the first cubicle, where a young woman sat typing furiously.

"Excuse me," I said, flashing my FBI badge. "Agent Slade. We're investigating a murder across the street, and I was wondering if you've seen anything suspicious lately."

The woman's face twisted in annoyance. "I'm Jade," she replied curtly, not bothering to turn around.

Ignoring her attitude, I pressed on. "So, have you noticed anything unusual happening in that alleyway?"

"Nope," she replied sharply without looking up.

I sighed inwardly and made a note to follow up later. "Thank you for your time," I said, turning to leave.

I knocked on the metal-framed entrance to the second cubicle.

"Good afternoon, I'm Agent Slade from the FBI. Mr. Dark gave me permission to ask questions as part of an investigation. Has anyone noticed anything strange in, or around, the alleyway recently?"

Four people turned to look at me. One of them removed his headset.

"Not really," he replied. "But I did watch the day you guys messed around with that dumpster down there. It didn't look very organized. Most of you just stood around, watching two or three people do all the work."

"Interesting," I said, and focused on the others, who had removed their headsets as well. "How about you? See anything suspicious?"

They shrugged and shook their heads, but a few darting stares they exchanged struck me as suspicious. I thanked them for their time and moved on to the third cubicle, which was empty.

From the various documents scattered about, it was clear that this office belonged to HR staff. A board displayed a calendar noting an interview scheduled with Australia three days before the last body was discovered. There was no name listed next to the appointment.

I went back to the previous cubical and asked, "Are you all from HR here?"

The same guy nodded. "We focus on different parts of the world." No one else spoke.

"Do you know who had an interview in New Zealand a few days ago?" I gestured toward the calendar.

The four colleagues in the cubical exchanged glances before the same guy spoke again. I had a feeling they'd been given a heads-up about my arrival. "That was Russell. Unfortunately, he died last week in a car accident. It must have been late, because he walked through a red light, or something like that."

I scribbled some notes on my notepad. "What is his full name?"

"Russell Wright. Everyone here liked him."

"Was anyone else working here at that time of night?"

One woman with short curly hair and a bright paisley scarf added, "Maybe the janitors? They usually come in during the evening hours."

"Do you know their names?"

"They usually change it up—work on different floors, or something like that."

"Fremont worked last night," said another voice. "I talked to him while he cleared the trash."

"Can you describe Fremont?"

"He's maybe fifty years old, dark complexion, a patch on one eye, said he lost it in the war. He's fun and makes everyone laugh."

I thanked them as I jotted everything down. It would be awful if this case came down to one of the janitors, but it was another lead. I went to the sixth floor, where a similar bunch of worker ants were scurrying about.

I went to the first cubical in the corner. "Excuse me, but—"

"Are you a lawyer?" the very thin Asian woman asked.

"Um, no, but I—"

"Then we don't have time for you. Sorry."

I showed her my badge. "Now do you have time for me?"

She closely reviewed my credentials. "How can I help you, Agent Slade?"

"I have access to the building for the purpose of investigating a murder that took place in the alleyway across the street several days ago. I'd like to interview the staff on this floor to see if they witnessed anything."

"We're all attorneys working either patent cases or global contractual issues. Our heads are buried too deep in paperwork to see some murder scene, but feel free to ask around. Don't be surprised if you get the same response."

I'd worked with attorneys before, but none as cold as her.

"Thank you," I replied, and walked toward the cubicles nearest the windows overlooking the crime scene. A man stood by a copier, printing stacks of documents. As I approached him, heads popped up over cubicle walls like groundhogs before disappearing again. Someone had definitely sent out the message I was here.

When I walked toward the cubicle near the window, an older woman greeted me. "Hello. My name is Samantha. How can I help you?"

"Hi, Samantha." I showed her my badge. "I'm Agent Slade from the FBI, and I'd like to talk to those of you who may have worked late on the evening prior to March 3rd, around 2:00 to 4:00 a.m."

"No one on this floor works after 5:00 p.m. Their jobs are stressful enough, so I ensure that everyone leaves by five so they don't burn out."

Over her shoulder, a woman in a janitorial uniform emptied trash cans into a larger one on wheels.

"Thank you, Samantha, for your time."

I strolled to the janitor. She was a Latina woman, perhaps in her forties, with her hair in a ponytail and an expression of numbness.

"Hello," I said as she pushed her trash cart toward me.

"No speak English," she replied.

I spoke into my translator app on my phone and showed her.

172

Estoy con el FBI. Tambien trabajas por la noche?

She shook her head. "No. *Solo días.*" I played it in English and read, *No. Only days.*

I fiddled with the app again. *Conoces a un conserje nocturno llamado Fremont?* I wanted to see if she knew anyone named Fremont.

"*No, señora. No conozco a nadie mas que a mi jefe, el Sr. Frederick,*" she replied, and I saw it translated. She only knew her boss, Mr. Frederick.

Dónde está la oficina del Sr. Fredick? the app asked for me.

"*No lo sé. Por favor, debo hacer mi trabajo,*" she replied. I didn't need the app to tell it was a plea to let her get back to her job.

I nodded, only to notice a simple but elegant Rolex on her wrist as she passed.

Why would a janitor wear a five-thousand-dollar watch while picking up trash? I suppose she could have inherited it, but still. Something felt off.

The seventh floor was as quiet as a morgue. The hallways had letters, and each door had a number, but someone had locked each room. They must be the classified rooms.

The eighth floor had a lobby desk with the name "Legislative Liaison" in bold chrome letters.

"Can I help you, Miss—"

"Agent Slade, with the FBI." I showed the young twenty-something woman my badge. She was exquisite with silky jet-black hair and cobalt-blue eyes that were quite similar to the front desk clerk's in Switzerland.

"How can I help you, Agent?"

"I'm investigating a murder that happened across the street a short time ago. I'd like to question some people on the floor to see if they witnessed anything suspicious. Let's start with you. What's your name?"

"I'm Leila, and I'm sorry, but I've been too busy to notice anything."

"Thanks, Leila. Do you work in the evenings, by chance?"

"Sometimes Mr. Dark asks me to be his assistant when Sueann cannot, and that requires staying up some nights."

I bet it does, I thought. But I didn't recall the name Leila on any trust funds, so she may be safe.

"What's your role here at Dark Enterprises?" I asked.

"I'm kind of a floater. Mr. Dark hired me to be the face of his International Relations department, so I welcome people to the floor, as I did with you."

"Is this a liaison to other countries, or do other countries have representatives working here?"

"Oh, we have many countries with company representation here. It's much easier to communicate with the liaisons in person than over the phone or in virtual meetings."

I took a shot in the dark, as she seemed to network with many in the company. "Do you happen to know a janitor by the name of Fremont?"

"Of course. He usually works at night, and he seems to know everyone very well. Why do you ask?"

I thought about how I wanted to answer. "He was working on the night of the murder. Do you know where the janitors' office is located?"

"Sorry, I don't, but if you need to contact the Crowned Prince of Saudi Arabia, I could help you."

"Thanks, I'll keep that in mind."

Walking through the foreign liaison floor was a bust. I was getting tired of using my translator app to ask everyone the same question, only to find out that no one knew anything.

The ninth floor appeared to be a room full of ceiling-high computer servers. A woman sat at a desk amid the metal towers, reading a book with a Bose headset over her ears.

When I tapped my ear, she rolled her eyes, as though she wasn't getting paid enough to take a question.

"Can I help you?"

"Are there any offices on this floor?"

She tilted her head and began to chew some gum she must have hidden in her cheek. "You're looking at it."

"Sorry, I'm on the wrong floor."

"Obviously," she replied and put her headset back on.

The next floor up was another cubicle farm, but here, everyone was once again diligently typing away at keyboards. There were signs on various walls that said Europe, Asia, South America, the Caribbean, and the United States. The person nearest me was a man, perhaps in his early twenties, with a mohawk and a black T-shirt.

When I tapped him on the shoulder, he said, "Yo, what's up?"

I showed him my badge and introduced myself.

"Wow, a Fed! Hey, I don't think you can arrest me for pot when I have a doctor's prescription and when I don't have any on me right now."

I smiled down at him, then glanced at pictures and figurines on his desk of marijuana and mushrooms and wondered how some people's life goals were to fry their brain as often as possible.

"I'm here with the permission of Mr. Dark," I said, struggling to keep a straight face. "I just want to know what the people on this floor do."

"Oh, yeah, well, we do accounting work. Each country works on accounts receivable and accounts payable for business dealings all over the world. Since I know a little Spanish, I'm doing South America. I'm looking forward to going to Colombia soon."

"That sounds wonderful. Do you know anything about the companies on the second, third, and fourth floors, by chance?"

"No, not me. The United States cubical takes care of that. I do pay an invoice for security work now and then, but not too often."

"What kind of security work?"

"Um, I don't think I'm supposed to say. Sorry, I know you're a Fed and all, and could maybe shoot me, but I really like this job. They don't ask any questions."

"What's in that back room?" I pointed to a door in the corner next to another access pad.

"Oh, that's for classified government work. I haven't worked in that room. I like it right here in South America."

"Okay, thanks. I appreciate your help."

When I scanned my card on the access pad, there was a buzz and a red light.

"Can I help you, Agent Slade?" I turned to see Sarah Hanvey-Dark behind me in a blue pantsuit, her hair up in a bun. She swiftly surveyed me up and down, like a drill sergeant walking up to a soldier for inspection.

"Mrs. Dark—I mean, Mrs. Hanvey-Dark. I wanted to see what was in this room and tried to see if my badge worked here." I glanced around the floor to see several heads peering over cubicles. They must have sent the word out for her to come down.

"That room is for classified government accounting, and unless you have an authorized need to know, with the appropriate security clearance, you're not getting in there."

"My apologies. I'll just continue interviewing those by the window."

"You will find that no one in this room stays here past 5:00 p.m."

"Perhaps you might know where I can find Janitor Fremont?"

Her eyes never left mine. Cold, steely eyes that said I should stand down, but there was no way I'd cower to her.

"Do you think I keep track of janitors in this company?" she said crisply. "There are dozens in this building."

"Thank you for your time," I said and headed toward the exit. But when I paused at the door, I saw Sarah talking to a female janitor. The janitor nodded, glanced at me, and then Sarah walked away.

Maybe Sarah had more insight into the janitors than she led me to believe.

The idea of an employee getting into a fatal accident at approximately the same time as the victim kept running through my head.

I went back to the fifth floor, hoping to find more information about Russell.

"Sorry to bother you again, but do any of you have a picture of Russell, or perhaps a social media link?" I asked the group in the joint cubicle. They were huddled together, reading something on one computer screen.

They exchanged glances as if they were trying to decide what to say.

"I apologize, but we don't have anything further," the woman on my left said with a furrowed brow.

"If you just have a photo, it would be incredibly helpful." I handed her my business card.

"Kate already said it: We know nothing else," said the older obese man with an embarrassingly obvious toupee.

Someone had obviously warned them not to talk to me any further.

After hours of dead-end investigation, I decided to take a break. Across the street was a bistro that advertised a Mediterranean salad, and my stomach was begging me to try it. After promptly ordering and paying, I looked up to see Kate—the woman I had given my business card to ten minutes ago.

Saying nothing, she placed something in my hand, quietly turned, and left.

I picked up the picture and leaned against a refrigerator containing soft drinks. It was a photo of the man I'd seen next to Jane Doe Blonde #2 on Dr. Jefferies's examination table. There was no way a simple car accident victim would have ended up there.

After walking out of the bistro, I looked up at the tall building that housed Dark Enterprises. The security company on the lower floor seemed worth checking out. If Wilson taught me anything, doped-up addicts might be a wealth of knowledge.

When I arrived, a beautiful woman of apparent Indian descent manned a desk within a glass enclosure. I raised my badge, and the loud clicking sound indicated the door had unlocked.

"Agent Slade. I'm here at the invitation of Mr. Trevor Dark. I thought I'd stop here and see if anyone saw anything suspicious in the alley across the street recently."

"I'm sorry, Agent Slade, there isn't anyone here at the moment."

She looked familiar, but I couldn't quite place her.

"No one's here? Who's the president of the company?"

"One moment, please."

She picked up the phone and dialed a number. I walked around to see Indian decor similar to that in the elevator. The narrow elephant planter was fascinating, as was the beautifully colored wall hanging with four wise men in various colored robes.

"Agent Slade, you were granted permission to walk back through the floor."

"Thank you, Miss . . ."

"My name is Tanja."

I intently stared at her. "Were you at the gala the other night?"

"Yes, I was. Did you enjoy it?"

That's a debate I'm still having.

"Yes, I did. I remember you, but where were you working? The evening seems a little hazy."

"I was serving drinks to the guests," she replied.

She was the cocktail server who had brought us the champagne. Did she know that the champagne was drugged?

"I remember now. Do I need a badge to get in?"

"The badge you received at security downstairs should work here."

I stared at her longer than I should have. Why did my badge for

Dark Enterprises work for this company? Unless this security company worked for Mr. Dark.

When I approached the first room, a woman emerged. It was the same Latina cleaning woman Mrs. Hanvey-Dark had been talking to upstairs.

"Hello," I said. Tanja had said no one was here.

The cleaning woman wore a look of surprise. "*Hola. No hablo inglés.*"

The room she'd exited was a locker room of sorts, like you'd see in a gym. The decor was fairly masculine, with charcoal-gray walls, dark wood trim, and a musky scent. It was immaculate, with shower alcoves along the wall, their curtains pulled to the side. Everything was spotless. In fact, it was the cleanest locker room I'd ever seen.

Past the showers was another door—locked. I thought my key worked here?

Back in the hallway, I tried another—also locked.

One more door at the end of the hall. It was another locker room, but this one was more feminine, painted in sage green with white trim.

This time, the door at the other end of the locker room opened.

The room was like something out of a bondage sex thriller. Cushioned benches lined most of the walls, and several padded sawhorse contraptions were in the middle, while the corners had tall constructed metal frames with dangling ropes.

What the hell? Was this—

181

"Oh, Jenna! Oh my God! What are you doing here? You missed a fabulous evening in here, but I'm sure Mr. Tall, Dark, and Mediterranean was just as fun."

Sueann had walked out of what seemed like a hidden door. The wood trim made a nice cover to hide the seams.

She stretched her arms out to hug me. "You missed a great afterparty!" She followed my gaze to the door. "Trevor uses this secret passage, so no one knows he's here and he can leave more discreetly."

"Where does it lead?" I asked.

"It goes to his office, and then to the loading dock in back."

"I thought this was a security company?" I asked.

"It is, kind of. Some people here work for Dark."

"What are you doing here?" I asked. It didn't matter why she was there, I needed to get her to safety. I had a bad feeling she was going to be next on the hit list.

"I was told to come meet a client. Are you my client? I really hope so. You're so very beautiful."

"Sueann, you need to get out of here. Come with me, your life may be in—"

The room went dark. I thought I heard the latch of a door closing.

"Uh, Sueann?" I couldn't see my hand in front of my face. I reached for my gun, but realized I couldn't shoot in the darkness.

"It's okay. The exit light illuminates where the woman's locker room is located."

I spun around, looking for the exit sign, but nothing.

I replied, "But I don't see a—"

Chapter 21

Sluggishly, I regained consciousness. My vision was clouded by a dark fog, and I could barely make out the garbled voices in the distance.

Then I saw it—my gun in my hand.

Fear coursed through me.

I frantically scanned the room and recognized the bed, nightstand, and the curtains in the window—I was in my bedroom, just inside the doorway.

Slowly, I rolled in an attempt to get up.

"Freeze! Drop that weapon!" a deep baritone yelled from behind me.

Before I could sit up, uniformed officers filled the surrounding space, weapons raised. Instinctively, I tossed my gun to the floor and mumbled, "I'm FBI Agent Slade. What's going on?"

One officer broke the icy silence and answered my question with two words: "She's dead."

Horror rushed over me. "Who's dead? Where?" I asked before being shoved face down on the floor. Cold handcuffs encircled my wrists.

Then came a chillingly deep voice above me. "Agent Slade? We're bringing you in for murder."

"Murder? Who was murdered, and where?"

The uniformed police officer read me my rights as I tried to figure out what was happening. The last thing I remembered was talking to Sueann, the lights going off in Dark's room, and then waking up here.

"The victim's driver's license says Sueann Parisi," someone called out.

"We're bringing you in, Agent Slade, for murder."

Confused, I shook my head while they pulled me to my feet. Sueann was lying on the bed, wearing the same cream-colored day dress as she had when I last saw her in Dark's room. Two bloodstains marred her chest. Next to her was a pillow with two holes in it also, likely used to muffle the sound of the gun.

"There are two empty brass casings over here, Sergeant," an officer said from near the closet door about five feet away. Just the right amount of distance if I were to have fired the gun from where I woke up.

I was in a state of shock. Someone must have hit me on the head, or drugged me, and brought us here before shooting Sueann with my gun. But why would Sueann have come to my house voluntarily? Did someone hold me up and use my hand to pull the trigger while I was passed out? Finding gunpowder residue on my hands would be the perfect setup.

When I arrived at the station, two officers escorted me to the forensics lab, where they collected a blood sample, swabbed my hands for traces of gunpowder residue, and placed me in an interview room. The room was small, with one windowed wall dividing it from another room on the other side. They secured my wrists to a metal loop in the center of the table with handcuffs connected to a steel bar—a situation I was getting tired of.

After what seemed like an eternity, an older Latino man wearing a white shirt and black trousers entered with a folder under his arm and a cup of coffee in hand. He sat opposite me and leaned back in his chair, studying me intently before finally opening the folder. He was familiar, but I couldn't place him. Perhaps we had both gone to some symposium or training in the past.

He slid a photograph of Sueann, alive and smiling in a sundress, toward me. Her beautiful blonde hair hung behind her ear while she posed for a gorgeous photo. "I'm Detective Rodriguez. Do you know this woman?" he asked.

I should have pulled her out that night at the gala. I nodded. "Yes, her name is Sueann Parisi. She works for Dark Enterprises, and I saw her earlier today."

He raised an eyebrow and slid photograph of Sueann's lifeless body across the table. Red circles of blood on the front of her blouse. A shock and awe tactic we also learned at the academy to help intimidate a would-be killer. "Where did you see her last . . . alive?"

Closing my eyes, I pondered how much of what I had seen would be beneficial. "I was at the building of Dark Enterprises in a room that resembled some BDSM dungeon in what was supposed to be a security firm. I saw her coming out of a false wall, telling me she was meeting a client," I said. "The lights went out, and then I woke up in my bedroom with my gun in my hand, surrounded by the police."

There was a long pause again as he evaluated my body language and facial expressions. Someone was undoubtedly running a facial heat map behind the mirror to determine my truthfulness. In fact, given the surrealness of what I had just said, I didn't know if I would believe me.

"Forensics is covering the house, but it looks like your service weapon shot Ms. Parisi in your bedroom."

The pause after that remark was deafening.

"Obviously, someone set me up," I exclaimed, struggling to open my hands as best as I could while being restricted. "They knocked me out and probably drugged me in that room at Dark Enterprises, then brought me back to my house, where someone killed Ms. Parisi with my gun."

"Why would someone want to go through all that trouble to frame you?"

I stopped myself from shaking my head for a second. I didn't want to tell them what I'd uncovered so far.

"I'm investigating multiple homicides that have ties to very wealthy and influential people. That's all that I can tell you right now, other than that I suspect Dark Enterprises is involved."

Detective Rodriguez stared at the table, tight-lipped. Then he stood and walked out of the room.

Sueann's photographs remained on the table. Her before and after. Inside I was an emotional wreck. I could have saved her. I should have saved her on the night of the gala, but I believed it would do more harm than good with the investigation. Besides, the money was still in her account, so I assumed there was more time. Nevertheless, if I had, she might be alive today.

Detective Rodriguez returned and stared at me for a moment, then unlocked the handcuffs from my wrists. I thought it strange, but as long as I was getting these cuffs off, I wouldn't ask any questions.

"I believe you, Agent Slade, but the evidence doesn't look good for you. I ask that you stay local."

The door opened again, and Kimmel appeared with a stern look on her face that made me reconsider leaving. "I'm from the local bureau, here to take custody of Agent Slade."

"I'm releasing her right now," the inspector shot back. "But the evidence we collected doesn't look favorable."

"I'll take responsibility for her," Kimmel said firmly.

The inspector removed the second cuff from my wrist.

"Thank you," I said, getting to my feet and trying harder to place

Rodriguez. I had seen him before, but I just couldn't remember where.

Rodriguez waved his hand. "Don't thank me yet. If the forensics report points to you, then I may have no choice but to bring you in."

Kimmel glared at the inspector. "You bring that report to me first."

When we got into her car, Kimmel sat silently, staring through the windshield for several moments. I needed her assistance now more than ever.

"Were you holding your service weapon when the police walked in?"

I faintly remembered seeing the gun in my hand as I tried to sit up. Worst-case scenarios filled my mind, knowing what a positive answer to that question meant. "Yes."

"So, what are the chances they'll find gunpowder residue on your hands?"

I had already thought about that, which could be the nail in my coffin.

"I believe that if someone went through the trouble to stage that, they would ensure I was holding the gun when it fired."

"Whoever set this up is very good, Jenna. I'll do my best, but need you to trust me."

I was toast. My only chance was Kimmel.

"I went to the security firm on the third floor of Dark Enterprises to ask questions. When I walked to the back offices, there was no security company but a large BDSM room with two locker rooms. When I walked in, Sueann, the deceased, was there, and she said someone had sent her down to meet a client. The lights went out, and the next thing I saw was the police coming into my house as I woke up in a confused blur." I thought about telling her what Sueann had told me regarding the Dark Room, but I wasn't sure it would help me right now.

"Were you hit in the head?"

I didn't recall an impact, and there was no lump. "I don't know, maybe, but I was out too long just for a head bump."

"Did they draw blood when they took you in?"

"Yes."

Kimmel nodded. "Good. Hopefully, that will show the drug they used to knock you out." She started her car and continued, "Let's go check out this security firm."

When we arrived at Dark Enterprises, it was about four hours since I'd last been there. I didn't have my Dark Enterprises badge, so I couldn't access anything. They'd likely taken it away after knocking me out.

We went to the third floor, where a different woman greeted us.

"I'm Special Agent Kimmel from the FBI, and I need to speak to whoever is in charge here."

"One moment, Agent Kimmel."

As the receptionist made a call, I whispered to Kimmel, "Nobody was on this floor except for a different front desk clerk, and a cleaning lady who works for Dark upstairs, and whom I saw speaking with Sarah Hanvey-Dark."

A middle-aged man in a blue business-casual suit came around the wall. "Hello, Agent. I'm David Parker, owner of Sahara Security Services. How may I assist you?"

What the hell?

"Is Tanja not working the front desk anymore?" I asked.

Parker looked at me, confused, then to the front desk clerk. "I'm sorry, I don't know anyone by that name working here."

Just as I was about to throw down the bullshit flag, Kimmel spoke out, "We just came from a murder scene, and there is a slight possibility that one of your rooms may have some potential evidence. Would you mind if we had a look?"

"Of course not. Let me guide you there myself. I'm sorry for the loss and will help in any way I can."

Kimmel looked at me for affirmation, and I nodded, but inside I was filled with rage. This was not the same scene as earlier.

"This is where we do our scheduling." He opened the door to what used to be a locker room but had transformed into an office with desks and chairs and people bustling about. "As you can see, coordinating security for sites around the world requires a team of dedicated personnel."

"No way! Lockers lined the walls. There were showers over by . . ." I walked toward the back of the room, where there was now a line of filing cabinets.

"What's behind that locked door?" I asked, gesturing toward the closed door.

"Our training room. It may not rival the FBI Academy's, but we do our best to train our security personnel."

He opened the door, and we stepped into the large room with mats and people engaging in fighting techniques.

I wanted to shout but knew better than to make a scene. There was no trace of the metal framework from before, yet the benches were still along the wall, filled with students waiting for their turn to practice.

I walked over to where Sueann had come out of the wall, and knocked, but I couldn't hear the dull sound I'd here if the other side of the wall was open.

"Is everything all right, Agent Slade?" Mr. Parker asked.

"How long have you been running this company, Mr. Parker?" Agent Kimmel asked.

I returned to Kimmel, fuming. The heat on my face had to be physically evident.

"Oh, about five years now. We've kept quite busy."

"Who's your prime customer?"

He paused briefly. "We service customers across the globe. However, our specific clients fall under confidential information."

"No surprise there," I muttered under my breath.

Parker smiled. "Is there anything else I can help with?"

"No. We'll be heading out now," Agent Kimmel said. "Thank you for showing us around your facility."

"My pleasure. Let me know if I can be of any more assistance."

We walked through the glass doors and into the elevator.

Once the doors closed, I exploded. "None of that was there last time! I swear! Many things were similar, but they added the desks, and people, and—"

"That's enough. I believe you, but we need proof of why someone would go to such lengths to do this to you."

I stared out the window of Kimmel's car, watching the blur of buildings pass by. "Sueann's name was on a hundred-million-dollar trust fund connected to Dark Enterprises. Her name was on the trust, and the names of the other Jane Does were on additional trust funds that had zero balances. Someone wiped out the accounts shortly after each Jane Doe was murdered."

Kimmel replied, "If the other modus operandi was to throw a strangled victim in a dumpster, then why do this with Parisi?"

"To get me off their back. I'm getting close."

"Where did you come up with that?" Kimmel snapped.

"I asked a cyber-inclined friend to run that audit information you gave me, through his channels as a favor. He uncovered all the connections of money from where it came from to who received it. And he had decoded the building supplies to reference arms sales."

"Do you have this information?"

"He said he would send me the info, and I was waiting to tell you when I received it."

"You need to get me that information as soon as you do. That may be just the thing to keep you from life in prison."

We stopped in front of the Marriott Hotel downtown. I looked around, and then at Kimmel.

"What are we doing here?"

"I want you to spend the night here and rest, Jenna. Tomorrow is another day, and we'll tackle everything then."

I patted myself down. "The police have my service weapon." Frankly, all I had was my wallet. Not even a toothbrush, but I could get that at the front desk.

"It's evidence in a homicide now." She reached into her glove box. "Here, take this one. Don't lose it."

She handed me a Glock 9mm. She wasn't the first agent I'd seen with a backup gun in their car, even though it was technically against the rules.

"And Jenna . . ." She waited for me to meet her gaze through the open door. "Don't make me regret this."

Chapter 22

The next morning, I was stepping into the taxi to take me home—where I intended to turn the house upside down looking for a passcode—when Wilson drove by the hotel.

Where is he going?

I redirected the taxi driver to follow his car instead.

Given the falsified records, they clearly had no intention on solving the Jane Doe case. So, what were they really working on, and was Porter part of it? I thought back to the many months of us hooking up and found it hard to believe he would be involved in anything nefarious.

I looked at my clothes and realized I hadn't changed them since yesterday. There were a few wrinkles, but they were holding up well. If not for the shower at the hotel, I'd be rancid by now.

"Stop here."

Wilson had stopped at a guard shack at Port Miami. The guard waved them through, and they drove toward the stockpiles of containers.

I waited until Wilson's car was out of sight, then got out of the taxi and paid the driver. Fortunately, I had the eighty bucks.

At the front gate, I showed my badge. "Hi. Agent Slade. I think my colleagues got here before I did. Do you know where they went?"

"Sorry, Agent Slade, I didn't see you pull up."

"Yeah, I got dropped off. I need to catch up with them before they leave."

"They went to the export dock," he told me. "Just turn right when you reach the water.

"Thanks!"

I slid my badge into my pocket and stepped into the massive shipping container yard, staying close to the wall of containers on my left as I made my way toward the water.

My throat tightened when I saw Wilson's car parked next to the containers, but there was no sign of him or Baxter. Hoping for somewhere to hide if they emerged, I searched for a gap between the containers, but the rusted metal boxes were in tight formation.

I leaned against a dull brown container with pockmarks of rust along the wall, and waited for any movement. Footsteps approached. I stepped into the sound as a man in a hard hat reached the corner.

"Excuse me!" I exclaimed.

"Oh, I'm sorry, are you lost? Can I see some ID?"

"Yes, I'm Agent Slade. I'm looking for my colleagues, but I seem to have lost them. I've never been here before."

I showed him my badge. He looked at it, and then at me. "I saw some guys in suits with the dock manager, Frank, about halfway down this row. Walk down the water and you should see them."

"Great, thanks for the help."

I strolled toward the front, then peered around the corner. Wilson's car was gone.

I ran toward where I last saw his car and saw an opening between containers.

And a door.

The lever in front was simple enough. I gently lifted it off the hook, and the door squeaked open, leading into a poorly lit container. There were desks and stacks of crates along the walls. Corrugated steel made up the walls, reflecting what little light came from outside. My bureau-issued flashlight handled the rest.

Filing cabinets lined the walls, and the stacked crates bore various markings, none of which I understood. A blue folder sat on top of a table, under which were a couple of tucked chairs. I opened the folder to find nothing inside. What the hell were they doing in here?

Two wooden crates by the table had the word "Nuts" painted on the top. I pulled at the top of one crate, but it was tightly nailed down. A small pry bar was on the table, so I grabbed it and got to work, careful not to chip any wood or bend a nail.

Shining my light inside, I saw a box full of small, shiny nuts that you would screw onto a bolt. Still, remembering what Hamilton told me about the weapons smuggling, I pried off the top completely.

When I pushed the nuts aside and reached deeper, I found a false bottom starting three-fourths of the way up the crate. There had to be some sort of handle. I needed to act fast, as someone could enter at any time.

Having no success, I took a picture of the nuts in the case, and then the bottom of the crate. Then I tried to lift one crate, but it was heavy to carry, so I set it down again. I needed something to help me move these.

Spotting a dolly along the wall, I brought it to the crates, lifted the top one, and set it in the middle.

Voices sounded outside.

I speedily rolled it to the other side of the room, hoping to hide behind a large crate, but there was no room to hide both it and me, so I swiftly jumped on top of the crate, hid behind the taller box, and turned off my flashlight.

The door squeaked open, and the room lit up with another flashlight.

"There it is."

The sound of footsteps walked toward me. I reached for my Glock and waited.

"How did we miss this one? Good thing the boss caught it, or we'd be in trouble."

"Nah, they keep these here to show our Fed friends what we're shipping so they can get it through smoothly."

"Wait, weren't there supposed to be two crates?" the other man asked.

They scanned the room with their flashlights. A beam of light glanced across the crate beside me as I pressed against the wall.

"They're just bullets. The way they waste bullets over there, no one will miss another thousand," the first man said. "Come on, let's get this to the ship with the rest of the crates."

The footsteps walked away, and the door shut.

Did he say bullets? Hamilton was right.

When I turned on my light again, I realized the second crate was gone.

Since I had no way to take the remaining crate with me without a car, I found a few pieces of cardboard to at least cover it a little. I'd try to come back for it later.

When I peeked outside, some dockworkers were coming my way. I took off running in the opposite direction.

"Hey! You! Stop! This is a restricted area!" a man's voice called out.

I dodged through a couple of open corridors and thought I was completely turned around until I saw the blue of the ocean.

I ran toward the water to get my bearings when a police cruiser halted directly in front of me. With her gun drawn, the officer darted out and leaned over the hood.

"Put your hands up!" she yelled out while talking into her radio. Calling for backup, no doubt.

How many times in a week can I get the police to arrest me?

Gradually placing my hands in the air, I called out, "I'm Agent Slade with the FBI!"

"Get on the ground, face down, legs apart!"

I complied and glanced behind me as a car pulled up. *Shit!* It was Wilson.

"Agent Slade," said Wilson. "I don't think I've ever seen you in this position. Shouldn't you be in jail for murder? I must admit, this is a good look for you. I can definitely see why Porter likes to tap that."

Fuck! They know about me and Porter? But I couldn't focus on that now.

"Shut up, Wilson, and tell this water cop who I am!" I spat.

"It's okay, Officer, she's with us," Wilson called out.

The officer put her weapon away. I got up and brushed the debris from my suit.

"Thank you."

"What are you doing here?" Baxter hissed.

"I stumbled on some important information, but when I got to the office, I saw you leaving. I tried to catch up but got lost here." *Sounded plausible.*

"What's this information, and how did you get here?" Wilson asked.

I continued to brush dirt from my pants while thinking fast. "I did some interviews at Dark's headquarters, with permission of Mr. Dark, and found out that one of the employees may have seen the last murder victim dumped in that dumpster."

"I thought I directed you to not go there."

"Kimmel told me to go ahead." I figured Kimmel might endorse this lie if it came to it.

Wilson shrugged with tight, pursed lips. "Great, let's bring him in for questioning."

"The only problem is . . . he was killed in a car accident on his way home early that morning."

"Then why are you coming to me with shit? Bring me something we can use," said Wilson. "Jeez, Slade, no wonder you'll be nothing more than a traffic cop. That is, if you're not in prison."

Shaking his head, Wilson got in the car while Baxter laughed and got in the passenger's seat.

This had turned out better than I thought. He bought my story and believed I was stupid. Perhaps I could use that in my favor.

Once they left, I walked out of the gate. The phone in my pocket buzzed. It was Kimmel—*Come into the office.*

After a fifteen-minute drive, the taxi dropped me off at headquarters. Wilson's car was already in the parking lot. He might have some suspicions of my following him, but I hoped my performance had created doubt.

Back on our floor, I headed to Porter with the intention of telling him to fuck himself. He was wearing a perfect poker face.

"Wilson, Slade . . . Come in my office," Kimmel barked.

When Baxter followed us in, she raised her eyebrows.

"Did I call your name?" she asked.

"No, ma'am." He stepped backward, and the door closed. Kimmel walked behind her desk and sat down.

"I feel the two of you aren't playing well together. Why?"

Before I could get a word out, Wilson replied, "To be honest, ma'am, I don't know why you appointed her to help me. She doesn't coordinate her work with me, she gets my orders overturned by you, she runs off on vacation to Europe, and she's been arrested for murder in her own home. I don't think she's even suitable to educate our youth anymore. Perhaps a crossing guard."

"You fucking—"

"Slade. Stop right there. I knew about her trip to Europe because I approved it, and the rest is being investigated. Keeping it civil, do you have a response to him?"

Where is she going with this?

"It's true, ma'am. I thought it wise to interview those who had a view of that alley and found someone who may have witnessed the body being dumped there, but he was suspiciously killed in a car accident on his way home."

"That doesn't sound much like a lead then, does it? I told her going there was a dead end," Wilson added.

"Shut it, Wilson. Your investigation hasn't produced any results either," said Kimmel. Was there anything else, Slade?"

There was a lot more, but I didn't know what to say in front of Wilson.

"There is a janitor named Fremont with a patch over his eye who the witness may have talked to before he died. I'm trying to track this Fremont guy down."

"Wilson, have you given Slade any tasks other than to read those poorly developed case folders?"

"No, ma'am, but it wouldn't matter since she does what she wants anyhow."

"As a case lead, I'd expect better of you. Take lead and task your subordinates, or I'll start micromanaging everyone. Now get out of my office."

Although I wanted to shut the door on Wilson, I left it open for him to follow me out.

"Slade. Since you've already started, I want you to continue interviewing the employees at Dark's headquarters and report back to me. If I'm not here, just wait for me. I don't need you to wander off and get arrested by the local uniforms—again."

"I no longer have an access badge."

The second I said it, I wished I hadn't.

"So, incompetence also? I don't know what Kimmel sees in you, but I'm getting tired of it."

As I waited for my computer to come up at a snail's pace, I

thought about Kimmel and what she was trying to do. Was she testing me not to disclose things to Wilson? Or maybe she had *wanted* me to disclose more, to see Wilson's reaction, and I'd blown it?

I opened my email and saw an announcement of the death of a fellow agent. Then I gasped.

Hamilton.

The statement said he'd died in his sleep from a cardiopulmonary embolism. The rest of the article cited his family and his graduation from the academy.

There was no way he died of natural causes. Someone had received a tip about his work.

The work he'd done for me.

I glanced back at Wilson, sitting on his desk and laughing with Baxter and Porter. Wilson looked to Porter, and then to me. Wilson said something to Porter, who just nodded and looked away.

If someone knew about Hamilton, then they must know what I'd uncovered. How was it that I was still alive?

I logged out and walked to the bathroom, where I wet a paper towel, walked into a stall, and placed it on the back of my neck. I thought about all that money my father had locked away, and the remaining credit in that hotel. I could just quit the FBI, change my name, and go into hiding. Then I thought of my father's work on this case, and how I felt he was driving me to complete it, whether he was alive or not. I had to see it through.

Once I got my breathing under control, I reemerged and went downstairs.

Becky Jefferies was at her desk in the basement, staring at her computer, when I knocked at the open doorway.

"Yes, Agent Slade. How can I help you?"

"That man down here last week, olive complexion with a goatee. Do you know his name?"

She squinted at me, likely trying to understand why I would ask for that information.

Dr. Jefferies replied, "His name was Russell Wright. We released him to his next of kin."

"Is there an autopsy report?"

"I don't think so. We stored him here until we could notify the next of kin."

"Then why was he on the examination table with his head exposed? You likely took some photographs, right?"

"Agent Slade, you'll have to discuss the matter with Agent Wilson. He's the one who brought him here. He said it was a hit and run, and we were to support the city coroner's office."

"So, you didn't go to the accident scene to get him?"

"No. Agent Wilson and Agent Baxter brought him here."

I stepped a little farther inside her office to glance at her desk. I hadn't gotten a good look at it when Wilson had assaulted her and then shooed me out. I saw a picture of her and my father at some dinner with wineglasses in their hands. He looked happy. I never knew.

"Is that my father with you in that picture?" Of course it was him, but I wanted to get an answer from her.

Jefferies turned over the picture so it laid face down on the desk. "It was a long time ago. Is there anything else, Agent Slade?"

"Yeah, where was the injury that killed Mr. Wright?" She thought for a moment. "I think it was blunt-force trauma to the back of the head."

"Is that type of injury commonly associated with a car accident?"

"It could be. If the car was low enough, it would hit the back of his legs and cause his head to impact the windshield."

"But that would cause significant injury to his legs, wouldn't it?"

"Possibly. Why are you asking about that?"

"Did you have a relationship with my father?" I changed topics quickly to gauge her expression better. If anyone knew the truth, she would.

"I . . . Your father and I were friends a while back."

"How did he really die?"

She looked around the room, then at a smoke detector on the ceiling. Her hands fell between her legs, and she pointed up with her thumb. A subtle reminder that her office was under surveillance.

"Your father died of asphyxiation, most likely by a rope," she said.

"But the report said it was suicide. How can you be sure?"

"That's how the report was written." She motioned her eyes upward again.

Nodding, I made a point to look at the murder mysteries on her shelf.

"I see you're a Tom Clancy fan?"

She laughed. "You'd be surprised by how many people try to mimic the murder of a famous author, and attempt to apply the strategy so they won't get caught. These books help provide an out-of-the-box perspective. I'm always at the Barnes & Noble whenever these authors' next books come out."

"Okay, well, if anything else comes to mind, please let me know."

I walked away, realizing what I needed to do.

It was four thirty, and my chai tea latte was nearly empty as I waited in the parking lot. Kimmel had let me borrow another bureau car.

Here she comes.

Becky Jefferies finally walked out of the building and made a beeline for her silver Toyota Camry. She stopped when she saw the note I'd put under her windshield wiper.

New John Grisham novel released today.

She looked around to see if anyone was watching. She wasn't

likely to see me from two blocks away, but the hook was hopefully set. It was cheesy to put a handwritten note on her windshield, but no one would know what it meant besides her.

At Barnes and Noble, I found my way back to the shelf with many murder mystery authors.

Picking up a James Patterson, I paged through it, only to find myself sucked in.

"That was quite creative," Dr. Jefferies whispered as she picked another book from the shelf. "I get an email whenever a new John Grisham comes out, so I realized it was your message to meet. How did you know he was my favorite?

"I didn't. I just picked one."

"So, what do you want to know? I don't have much time."

"Everything you know. Was my father murdered, were there drugs in those women's blood tests, were the legs of that Russell guy damaged, and were you involved with my father?"

"You're in grave danger, Jenna, for asking such questions. I'm monitored all the time. I'm almost certainly being monitored right now."

"There's no camera access down this aisle. I checked. You can live with this information until you die, or you can make a difference. A good friend of mine from the academy just died for helping me. I'm gaining a lot of information, and I need those answers."

She paged through the book, perhaps glancing at words, but not reading. She slowly shook her head in a manner that made me think she wouldn't answer. She was scared, and I was likely putting her in a worse position.

"Yes, your father and I were romantically involved. He was more married to his work, and I was . . . well, I was just married, but I loved him nevertheless. He had pancuronium bromide in his system. It's a neuromuscular blocking agent that pretty much turns someone into a vegetable. He didn't have enough in his system to stop his organs, but there was enough to where he wouldn't resist someone hoisting him in a noose and leaving him there to die without the need to bind his wrists."

"So, did you do an autopsy on him?"

"No. I just . . ." She paused. "When your father was brought in, I took a blood sample, and then he was taken away immediately."

"Did he have a pulse?"

She paused. "I don't know."

"How can you not know if he had a pulse?"

"Because the drugs in his system could have slowed his heart rate to nearly zero, but he could have recovered from it. They took him away before I could conduct further evaluation. I was just directed to sign the death certificate."

I was about to ask her where they took him when she added, "You'll have to ask Scelisi about anything further. I've already told you too much."

My eyes widened as I stared at the blurring letters before me—

Scelisi. "Why didn't you report it?"

"Agent Wilson threatened to tell my husband about my affair with your father. My husband was in the DEA, and was killed last year during a sting operation."

"I'm sorry about your husband. Is Agent Wilson blackmailing you? Why?"

"Wilson might be hard-lined under Kimmel, but he follows a different leadership structure. Let's just say the kind that can make people disappear without a trace. They forced me to cover up the drug use in the Jane Does as well. When my husband died, I was going to bring everything out in a report, but Wilson explained how I would go to prison, or worse."

"You were blackmailed, so you may face less severe consequences. Was there a particular drug found in those women?"

"There were traces of flibanserin and bremelanotide with a hint of theobromine. It's the ultimate date rape drug, as it significantly increases a woman's sexual desire while also stimulating her like speed. It would turn the most devout nun into a wanton whore within an hour."

"How is it taken?" I recalled my evening at the gala, where, if it had not been for Mr. Mediterranean, I may have been in a worse situation.

"It can be in many forms."

"Can it be in a drink?"

She thought momentarily. "Sure, it's possible, but it would most likely require something bubbly, like champagne, as it may not break down like other powders."

"Is any of this documented anywhere? You've got to have a fail-safe; otherwise, what's keeping them from killing you?"

"I do, and I believe it's keeping me alive right now." She closed her book and placed it back on the shelf. "Jenna, I truly loved your father. He was a good man, but he got too close to the truth. He was deeply undercover with the same group Wilson is in, and he downloaded a lot of data that would blow the lid off the entire global operation. I'm talking politicians, world leaders, billionaires, and terrorists. He was close to exposing everything, and I believe no one wanted to take any chances, so they killed him, and I fear the same for you if you get any closer."

I knew she didn't want to risk staying any longer, because she kept looking behind her whenever she heard footsteps.

"I have one more question before you leave," I pressed.

"Hurry, what is it?"

"What does Dark Enterprises have to do with all this?" She shook her head and looked down. "You've told me so much already. I really need this."

"They are central to all the money and global logistics operations for the entire thing. I can't answer anymore. I've gotta go."

She put on her sunglasses and walked away. Images flashed through my mind of that night at the gala when Sueann was enticing me to go to Dark's room. Given the way I was feeling from the drug,

I just may have . . . and then what? Would I have been found in a dumpster the next morning, or blackmailed to turn over what I have?

I was walking out the door when a nearby explosion knocked me off balance.

"No, no, no, no . . ."

My impulse drove me to run toward the smoke and flames as everyone else fled, only to find what remained of Dr. Jefferies's silver Camry.

Flames billowed out of the shattered windows. In the driver's seat was only the silhouette of a body.

Chapter 23

looked around the parking lot to find anyone watching suspiciously from a car, but saw no one. I looked at Dr. Jefferies one more time, took a deep breath, and walked away. Guilt consumed me, my heart raced. She died because of me.

I would only put myself in further danger if I were found here with her, but the fact that they killed her meant they knew she talked with me.

My hand trembled as I picked up a tumbler to pour some bourbon, barely able to keep it all in the glass. Then I downed it in one gulp.

My mind raced as I returned home. I was terrified for my own safety after what had happened to Dr. Jefferies in the middle of the day. If they could do that, who knows what else they could do?

"Shit!" I yelled out loud, with only silence to follow.

I was pouring another bump of golden courage when my pocket buzzed. I pulled out the burner phone and saw it was from Kimmel.

"Agent Slade? Are you all right?" she asked, giving me pause.

Ah, crap. She's been tracking this phone!

I took a deep breath to regain my composure. "Of course. Why do you ask?"

The response came slower than usual. "Jenna, I need to see you in my office at seven o'clock tomorrow morning."

"Yes, ma'am," I answered obediently.

The call ended abruptly, and I stared at the phone. Why had she really given me this phone?

I finished off my second drink in one gulp and grimaced as the alcohol seared my throat. Suddenly, Dr. Jefferies's words about a fail-safe came back to me—she mentioned having all the evidence somewhere. Why would they have killed her if she had hidden it? Where could it be?

I added more bourbon to my glass and walked into the kitchen, needing something stronger than bourbon to calm me down. On the way, I checked the window. No black car was visible, so I opened the freezer and spotted chocolate chip cookie dough ice cream—in all probability, the only edible food left in my fridge.

I grabbed a spoon and settled on the couch to mindlessly watch some news. I'd typically scan through multiple media outlets, but Sean Murphy was usually the most trusting source of information, especially when it came to government corruption.

I was halfway into my small dish of delight when it hit me. John Grisham. She mentioned he was her favorite author in the bookstore. Did someone else hear her say that?

I couldn't wait until morning to find out. I slipped on my shoes, donned my spare shoulder harness and the gun Kimmel gave me, slipped into my jacket, and left.

The steel double doors at the back of headquarters led to the medical examiner's room. When I arrived, one of the double doors was cracked open.

Pulling out my gun, I used it to open the door far enough to step through.

Alarm bells rang loudly in my mind as I tiptoed down the dark, silent hallway. I intentionally didn't use my flashlight in order to keep my presence unknown.

The silence was deafening as I got closer and closer to the exam room. The only sound I heard was my heartbeat—at least until a thud sounded from the other side of the wall.

Someone was in Dr. Jefferies's office. Were Jefferies's killers in there looking for the same thing I was?

Another thump rang out, sounding like something hard had landed on the floor.

A light flashed, and then someone whispered. "Got it!"

Grabbing my flashlight, I turned around the corner with the light guiding my gun barrel.

"Stop where you are!"

A shot rang out in a fraction of a second and hit the wall next to me. I shot toward the origin of the muzzle flash as another rang out, grazing my arm. I shot at that flash also, and then silence filled the room again.

When I flipped the light switch, Wilson and Baxter were lying on the floor.

"Fuck! Shit! Damn it!" A wave of swear words flew out of my mouth as I realized I had shot my FBI colleagues in the FBI detachment.

My heart was beyond racing as I holstered my gun and checked on Baxter, placing my fingers on his neck. He had no pulse.

Then I stepped to Wilson, who was staring up at the ceiling blankly. His chest was heaving, and he was making a terrifying gurgling sound. Blood spilled out of his mouth.

Feebly, he reached up with a key in his hand. He tried to talk, but only coughed up blood.

The smell of sulfur in the air only enhanced my panic. Blood spatter covered the shelving behind them and was now running on the floor like spilled coffee.

What the fuck did I just do?

Tears filled my eyes. I didn't care for either of these assholes, but I couldn't help but feel guilty. Why had they shot at me?

Wilson struggled as he held a hand with the key closer. I looked into his eyes as he nodded and motioned his hand again. I took the key just as his head and hand fell to the side. A John Grisham book lay next to him.

I looked at the tiny key, small enough to be for a Barbie house, or a locket, or something. I searched around and stopped at the picture of Becky and my father. There was a small hole at the top of its frame. I looked down at the key and back at the hole again.

It can't be that easy.

I placed the key in the small hole and turned it. The upper part of the frame popped open, exposing a small chip, the kind you'd find in your cell phone.

The lights in the exam room turned on, and the sound of many running steps grew louder. I hurriedly placed the key and the chip in my jacket pocket, locked the frame, and waited for what was sure to happen next.

"Freeze!" a man's voice called out.

I raised my arms. "I'm Agent Slade."

"I'm sorry, Agent Slade, but I'm going to have to cuff you until we figure out what happened here," the security officer exclaimed.

I nodded and placed my hands behind my back. "It's all right. I'm getting used to it."

He patted my jacket and removed my service weapon, then guided me out of the room to a chair in the examination room.

I sat for what seemed like hours as the examination room filled with agents and another medical examination team, each looking at me with undisguised disdain. I watched them mindlessly, not hearing a sound, as faces looked toward me, then turned to whisper.

"Slade! What the hell happened here?" Kimmel walked up to me with her hands on her hips.

"Do you know why they were down here?" I asked defiantly.

"Don't you fuck with me, Slade. You killed two FBI agents inside this FBI building. My building. Explain!"

I knew I could trust her, but with Jefferies concerned about the lab being bugged, I didn't want to take a chance.

"Dr. Jefferies had some mystery novels down here she said I could borrow at any time. I couldn't sleep, so I came down here and heard a commotion with flashlights shining around. When I turned the corner, I ordered them to freeze, but they both shot at me, so I fired back. I didn't know who they were until I turned on the light."

She looked at me with pursed lips. "I know you can lie better than that."

She walked to the office entrance and talked to one of the other agents. He pointed to a hole at the doorway, and another at the edge of the door. When she looked back at me, I saw her mouth a thank-you to the analyst next to her.

Kimmel gestured at the security guard to follow her, then returned to my side. "Take off the handcuffs," she said, and I turned so the guard could more easily remove the restraints.

"It seems like you went to the range more than they did," she added. "I still don't believe you came here for a book. What did

Jefferies tell you?"

"Have you been tracking me?" No sugarcoating or beating around the bush. I was done with tap-dancing. I'd nearly gotten killed tonight.

"Bryce," Kimmel said to the guard, not taking her eyes off me. "You can leave us now."

After he walked away, she whispered, "This entire building is bugged, and yes, I'm keeping tabs on you; your situation is too dangerous. I'm your only chance of staying alive and discovering the truth."

"What truth?" I whispered back.

She looked at me, carefully considering her words.

"All the truth, the truth I hope you got from Switzerland, the truth you got from your father, the truth you got from Jefferies . . . All of it, so we can put a lid on the whole damn shit! I want all of it brought to my office tomorrow morning. Understand? All of it!"

"I—"

"Unless your next words are 'yes ma'am,' don't say another word. Just get out of here and be in my office with everything you have at 7:00 a.m. I'll be lucky to still have this job at nine, so we need to see what you have without delay."

"You're getting fired?"

"Do you think a station chief can remain in place while her medical examiner gets blown up, and one of her agents shoots two of her other agents in one day?"

"She can if we prove they were part of some corruption."

"Bring the evidence, Jenna. Bring the evidence. Oh yeah, and Jenna? If you're going to shoot someone, make sure you don't have alcohol on your breath."

When I remembered the copious amounts of bourbon I had drank before entering this building, my entire body seized up in panic. How could I have been so careless? But there was no way I expected someone would try to shoot me. What else could go wrong?

As Kimmel made her way toward the elevator, I wondered if I had really cost her, her job.

Wilson clearly had something to do with Jefferies's death. He must have tapped into her voice-monitoring system on her cell phone somehow. Pulling off something like that would take some serious government clearance. Like some sort of Patriot Act approval, but that would need to be done at very senior levels.

Reaching into my pocket, I pulled out the key and computer chip. As I stared at the new pieces of evidence, I couldn't help but wonder how much more there was to find.

Chapter 24

Back at home, I stared at the bourbon bottle, my tumbler beside it. How could I have been so stupid? Then again, it did make one thing clear: If Kimmel was against me, she would have had me in cuffs by now.

Tomorrow, everyone in the FBI would know that I killed two of their colleagues. There would be no coming back from that.

Thinking about how someone could monitor Dr. Jefferies, I looked at the alarm panel by the door, and suddenly became enraged at the thought that they were watching me too. I sprinted toward the hall closet and grabbed a hammer, pried open the security control panel by the front door, then did the same to the back door. Unable to leave any device behind that I had no control over, I went through each room, ripped off the smoke detectors, and placed them all in a kitchen drawer.

My phone started ringing. "Hello, Ms. Slade. Your alarm system seems to have been tampered with. Shall we contact the authorities?"

"No! Just shut it down!" I shouted. "I don't need it on for a few days."

The muffled sound of the detector chirping in the drawer was beyond annoying. I grabbed a trash bag and tossed all the gadgets inside before dumping it into the trash can out back. When my gaze shifted, I saw the black car between houses. Instantly, I sprinted toward it. But within seconds, its taillights lit up and disappeared on the road before I could get a good look at the plates.

Doubt overcame me like an ominous storm cloud. It couldn't have been Wilson, because Wilson was dead. Scelisi?

"Jenna, is everything all right?"

Kenny was standing in his doorway with a baseball bat, prepared to fight off any potential threat.

"No . . . I mean . . . yes." I sighed. "Everything is fine, Kenny." The last thing I wanted to do was be the cause of his heart attack.

"Would you like to come inside for some tea?" he asked.

It was already past three in the morning, and I had to get some sleep.

"Thank you for your help, Kenny, but I need to get home. You're very sweet."

"If you ever need any protection, just let me know," he replied, slapping his bat.

I couldn't help but smile as I returned home. Perhaps I should spend more time with Kenny. After all, I had promised him that I would.

When I returned to my house, I saw a FedEx man climbing into his truck.

"Wait!" I sprinted to him. "Do you have a package for Jenna Slade?"

"Yes, I have a high-priority package. Just need to see some ID before I can give it to you."

I gave him my badge and FBI identification. He looked at my ID, and then at the screen of his handheld computer.

"I guess that will work. Here's your package. Just sign here."

"I didn't think you delivered at this time of the day, or night."

"We do for some priority packages. The person who sent this paid to deliver it immediately upon arrival."

I signed his little digital machine and walked inside, then froze when I saw it was from Hamilton. I didn't think he'd mailed it before he died.

I ran up to my old bedroom, where the rest of my evidence was hidden, and opened the package. It was a thick bundle of paper, perhaps one hundred pages thick. A letter from Hamilton was attached to the front.

Jenna,

There is a lot of danger with this information. I see many powerful people all over the globe in this document. I detected that someone had gained insight into my research, most likely putting me in jeopardy. I think I'll go on vacation for a few weeks in case anyone is suspicious.

Be careful, Jenna, and I look forward to that rain check.

Hamilton

The coolness of a tear rolled down my cheek as I perused through the pages, seeing one name in abundance—Dark. I cast my gaze around my old bedroom, bringing back memories of school achievements, like track and volleyball awards. Despite being swamped with work, Dad always made time to see me receive them.

I went to my nightstand and opened the music box he had gifted me for my twelfth birthday, when I returned from summer camp. It was where I kept all my small trinkets to include the thumb drive with the family photos. Inside was a beautiful dancing figurine, as well as an extravagant bronze coin etched with an image of me and him. He'd said if there was ever a loud commotion in the house, I should take that coin and place it in the middle of the narrow wall in the closet. When he did it, the wall opened to a small hiding spot not much bigger than to fit my twelve-year-old self. I would barely fit in that small space now, but my recent evidence fit in there nicely, along with the newest addition from Hamilton.

I was supposed to turn everything over to Kimmel in the morning, and yet, I couldn't help but feel that my father's work would be lost if I did. I didn't even look at what was on that hard drive from Switzerland since I still hadn't figured out the passcode.

The thunderous pounding on the door reverberated through the house like an earthquake, sending a shock wave of fear through me. I carefully shut the secret door and thrust the coin deep into my pants pocket before peering out of the bedroom window.

In the driveway was a menacing black Dodge Charger.

Grabbing my gun, I carefully crept downstairs to the front door. I could see nothing through the frosted-glass panels other than a mysterious figure. With gun cocked and ready, I unlocked the door and pulled it open with a sudden jerk.

"Don't you dare move!" I shouted.

It was Scelisi. He gradually raised his hands. An initial look of wide-eyed horror was on his face, and then calm.

"Just stay still." I reached inside his tweed jacket and gently pulled out his firearm. "Now walk slowly into the living room, and keep your hands visible."

He did as instructed, and then asked nervously, "Jenna, this isn't funny. What's going on?"

After patting him down and confiscating yet another weapon from an ankle holster, I ordered him to sit down in the living room. Then I proclaimed, "If you want to help me, tell me no more lies— everything. The truth about fucking everything!"

"I heard about your incident with Wilson and Baxter. How are you holding up?"

"I'll ask the questions. What did you know of my father going to Switzerland?"

"We went there a few times together, but he would go alone once or twice a month."

"Why?" I kept my gun pointed at him while standing about ten feet away. If he were to lunge for me, I'd be prepared.

"Jenna, there are some things you're better off not knowing."

"Is it you who's been spying on my house? Spying on me?"

He paused. "Yes, but only to protect you."

"Bullshit. your protection knocked me out and put me in the hospital."

"I'm sorry about that. You weren't supposed to be hurt. My partner got a little out of control."

"So, that was you searching my house when I walked in?"

"Jenna, your father and I were deep undercover in a global corruption enterprise. They would pay tens of thousands of dollars for assistance with security operations, or to grant approval for certain shipping containers to be imported or exported. He was compiling intelligence of the entire worldwide organization. When they found out, they killed him."

"What did the vice president have to do with this? What did my father do with him, and what are you doing with him?"

"I can't answer those questions, Jenna."

My rage overwhelmed me. "You're in on all of this, aren't you? Wilson and Baxter worked for you, didn't they?"

"Jenna, I . . ."

"Tell me the fucking truth!" Showing my firm grasp on my gun, my arms stiffened, and I wasn't sure myself if I would pull the trigger. "Baxter and Wilson were in self-defense. You would be breaking and entering, and I was startled. At least that's what I'd tell the police when they find you dead."

His face showed no emotion, no concern. Then he slightly nodded in contemplation. "Your father is still alive," he whispered.

My entire body softened. I lowered my arms and looked into his eyes. "You're lying. Dr. Jefferies said you brought him into her exam room and found some long-named drug in his system after taking a blood sample. Did you give that to him before you killed him?"

"She gave me the drug."

A hurricane of emotion and confusion ran through my mind. I didn't know what to think. There was no way he was still alive. I saw his autopsy pictures. But then again, there was nothing else in his report.

"Where is he?" I couldn't help but think this was some ploy to take my guard down.

"I don't even know, but he's been looking out for you since his death, or fake death."

I stopped my head from shaking in disbelief. "Oh my God, Scelisi, if you're lying to me . . ." A salty tear ran into the corner of my mouth. "Why are you really here tonight?"

"I'm trapped, Jenna. Your father and I worked for Vice President Brandon for years, even back when he was a senator, funneling weapons to countries that shouldn't have them, escorting Dark Enterprises so their logistics process went smoothly. Many powerful people have become enriched from it."

"You didn't answer my question. Why are you here tonight?"

"I need what evidence you have. My life and your life depend on it."

I shook my head, my gun pointed at his center. If he so much as twitched, I was going to shoot him.

"Who else knows my father is alive?" More tears ran down my cheek. I brushed them away on my shoulder. "Who!"

"I'm the only one who knows. Well, me and Becky, but she's dead now. I gave him a drug that slowed his heart rate and set him up in a rope so his neck would have rope marks. I let him down before it was too late and staged the rest of the scene to make it look like suicide."

I wanted to pull the trigger right there. I had no idea what was preventing me from that little nudge of my finger. "Where is he?"

"I don't know. After we revived him, he was supposed to take the money and run. He had a hefty sum of cash. But you know that already, don't you?"

I thought about the millions of dollars in cash in that vault, and then the line of credit in the hotel. Could he have taken some money to live on? But those pictures—they seemed so real. He had to be dead . . . didn't he?

"What roles did Wilson and Baxter have in this?"

"They, too, were involved, but reported directly to Mrs. Dark."

"You mean Mr. Dark?"

"I mean Sarah Hanvey-Dark. She runs everything. Trevor Dark is simply a womanizing figurehead. Many foreign people will only work with a man, so Sarah uses him as she needs to."

"So, this Dark Room has nothing to do with Trevor Dark?"

"Oh, I'm sure he plays around in there, but he's just a pawn. In my opinion, he's the fall guy if this entire thing goes down. But Jenna, we can't be hasty. We need to find all the evidence and secure it. So please, where is it?"

"That night at the gala, did you know what they do in Dark's room?"

"Yes, I knew, but I didn't care what they and their clients did. I was trying to prevent you from getting drugged and taken there."

"Why did you threaten Donte?"

"Because he's a global womanizer, and I didn't want to see you get hurt."

"What's Kimmel's role in all of this?"

"She's a clueless shell who just wants to survive until retirement and looks the other way most of the time. She serves no purpose other than to sign paperwork."

Based on her support of me, I didn't believe this.

"Who killed those women found in the dumpsters?"

"I don't know, Jenna."

"Did you know that each of their first names are the same names on trust funds in the Caribbean? They were primary beneficiaries on the trust, but once they died, all the beneficial interest was divided among everyone else? They used these women and let them think they were getting wealthy while role-playing as Trevor Dark's mistress and whores for his guests. Then, once the funds reached a hundred million, they killed them. They picked attractive women who had no family to be concerned if they disappeared."

The sound of shattering glass startled me, followed by a searing burn on my arm. Wincing in agony, I whipped around just in time to see Scelisi leap at me. My hand snapped out instinctively, and I fired a shot, only for another to echo back, making more of the window glass explode into shards. Someone was shooting from outside.

I scrambled frenziedly across the room, my feet kicking up pieces of glass that clung to my skin like needles. Blood spilled down my arm, staining my shirt and dripping to the floor. I could feel that the bullet had gone through flesh but not bone.

Scelisi yelled, "She's down the hallway! Don't kill her!"

Damn, he's still alive.

My heart pounded as I raced into my father's office and slammed the thick wooden door behind me. Panic swelled within me as reality hit—there was no way out. Blood gushed from my arm wound, and I knew if I didn't treat it soon, I'd pass out from shock and blood loss.

In desperation, I grabbed an expensive bottle of scotch and poured it all over the gunshot, grimacing as it soaked into the wound. Reaching for a clean bar towel draped on the bourbon table nearby, I bit down hard and tore it into several strips with my teeth before tying them tightly around my arm in a makeshift tourniquet.

This seems much easier in the movies.

A shadow passed by the window. Then a silhouette stood by the glass, looking inside with what appeared to be infrared goggles.

I held the gun and dropped behind the desk.

Shattering glass reverberated through the room, followed by the crunching of boots on broken shards. I lunged over my desk and fired toward the assailant, clad in all-black tactical gear. He fell back against the wall, hastily returning fire. My heart raced as I realized his vest was bulletproof—I had only seconds before he would be back up again.

Sliding under the desk, I used all my senses to pinpoint his location. Aiming at the thin wooden front of the desk, I opened fire.

Click click click.

Shit. I was out of ammo. Panic set in as I fumbled for an extra magazine, only to realize that I had failed to reload more than the one bullet after removing the vault key earlier.

Chambering the last round, I waited in deafening silence. Suddenly, there came a banging on the door.

"Jenna, open up. I won't hurt you," Scelisi called out.

I remained silent and waited for my chance to act. Peeking around the side of my desk, I saw a dark figure slumped against the wall, his weapon laying on the floor. I couldn't tell if he was breathing or not.

Taking a deep breath, I crept forward to investigate. One of my shots had hit him in his IR goggles, going through and piercing his head. Kneeling beside him, I strained to detect any signs of life, but there was no pulse.

But this fight wasn't over yet.

I pulled off his goggles and mask and gasped in shock—Porter.

"No, no, no," I quietly exclaimed as I stumbled away from his unmoving body. I remembered all our previous encounters. How could he . . .? Perhaps that was why he'd been so distant lately; he must have known something like this could happen. Confusion and emptiness spun through my mind.

"Jenna, come out and let's talk!" Scelisi called through the door as he rattled the knob. The police would arrive soon, and I couldn't risk being jailed for even a few hours. Movies were made of stories like this, and they always ended up with someone committing suicide in a jail cell while the cameras weren't working.

I grabbed Porter's service weapon and scrambled out of the office window, trying to minimize the crunch of shattered glass. When I peeked inside the window at the end of the hallway, there was Scelisi with a gun. So much for wanting to talk. He put his phone up to his ear and began speaking, revealing a smear of blood on his shirt and jacket—I must have shot him in the side.

The sound of blaring sirens grew louder.

Two unmarked cars pulled up in the front of the house with a screeching halt. I ducked behind the bushes as six men jumped out and ran to the house.

I crept around the corner, heading to the back. Still bleeding like this, I'd be caught for sure before I even got three blocks away. I didn't want to hurt anyone else, but it was time to visit a neighbor.

"Jenna! Are you all right?" Kenny asked when I rapped on his back door.

"Let's go inside and get away from the windows," I replied.

"Yes, yes, come in."

Kenny glanced around before shutting and locking the door behind us.

"Just wait here. I'll grab a first aid kit from the kitchen and turn off any lights so nobody can see us."

When he returned, he automatically went into medic mode. "I heard shots nearby. Who shot you?"

"It's a long story, Kenny, but I'd really appreciate it if you could help me with this wound."

He smiled. "Sure thing. Back in Korea, they trained me to be a medic. Before that, they tested if we could stomach cutting open a pig carcass. Luckily, I passed that one."

"You're kidding, right?"

Kenny laughed as he cut some gauze tape. "Yeah, you got me, but you'd be surprised how many people believe that story."

Soon enough, he declared it finished and showed me the neatly wrapped bandage.

We both looked out of the windows for any signs of movement.

"Thank you, Kenny."

"You're welcome. Now let's go crack some skulls," he said as he grabbed his baseball bat from the wall by the front door.

I stopped him.

"Kenny." I was grateful for his eagerness to help me, but I couldn't get him hurt. "The police will come looking for me. I don't want you to get in trouble, or hurt. I'll leave as soon as I catch my breath."

"Nonsense. I've never been so alive in almost twenty years. I've got your back, Jenna. I'll stand guard until morning, then we can see about cracking some skulls. Do you want to sleep in my bed? I'll make some coffee and stand watch," he asked.

"I'll just nap on the sofa with the blanket and pillow there—I'll be fine."

"Okay. We'll maintain complete blackout, and I won't let anyone get near you. Get some sleep."

I strode to the couch and set my gun on the end table as my heart thumped like an old engine. I thought of Scelisi saying Kimmel was not involved. This was reassuring. And what about my father being alive? Could it be true? And Scelisi had shouted not to kill me. Did he say it just to get the evidence easier?

Damn it. The drop phone.

I switched off the GPS services just as a text came through from D.

Are you okay?

My fingers flew over the keys as I replied, *I'm all right. Hitched a lift and found shelter. Scelisi and Porter made an attempt on me. Not sure what to do.* Hopefully, I had turned off the tracking soon enough.

Shortly after, another message came through. *Rest at your current spot for the night. I'll give you instructions tomorrow. Did they get the evidence?*

Unknown but doubtful, I tapped back.

Stuffing the phone into my pocket, I grabbed a blanket and snuggled up with a pillow before giving one last look around.

My medic was in the kitchen, wearing a bathrobe, with a slight hunch in his back, making coffee, and ready to guard me all night.

Chapter 25

"Jenna . . ."

I burst up in a panic, reaching for my gun, but it was just Kenny holding a cup of coffee while dressed in khakis, boots, and a flannel shirt.

My heart slowly settled. "Oh, Kenny. What time is it?"

"It's six thirty. I figured you'd want some caffeine before the morning came."

"Thank you, that's very considerate of you." I took a sip, and the strength popped my eyes wide open.

"I learned to take coffee black when I was twelve, working at a grain mill before school, but I have cream and sugar if you like?"

"Thank you, Kenny. Black is just fine." I took another sip and was nearly fully alert. "Did you stay up all night?"

"Damn straight I did. I told you I would keep you safe. I don't think that coffeepot has seen as much action in years."

I laughed. "Thanks for that. I'm glad this is where I ended up."

He asked me about the plan of action. The lights remained off as I moved to the window and looked outside. Police officers wandered around with their flashlights, blue and white lights flashing on their parked squad cars. Finding another dead FBI agent and an injured senior agent wouldn't look so good right now.

Still, they probably wouldn't recover anything else. My father built that secret compartment well enough that no one could find it.

My drop phone vibrated.

Senior reps from DC have come down to investigate this case. It's too risky for you to return now. Stay hidden until I give you the okay.

A sudden knocking startled me. Kenny gestured to his bedroom, so I dashed in, then placed my ear against the door.

He opened the front door and spoke to someone outside. "Hello."

"Good morning. We're searching for an armed fugitive and cop killer in the vicinity. She's armed and very dangerous."

Kenny snapped back with a huff, "You bastards recruited me for 'Nam but didn't even use me! No way am I joining you now to go on patrol!"

I almost burst out laughing.

"Thank you, sir. If you see anything suspicious, or a woman looking for help, please call 911."

"Me and my Louisville Slugger can take care of ourselves," he said before shutting the door.

After a few moments had passed, I walked out of the bedroom.

"How did I do?" Kenny asked.

I smiled. "You were brilliant! Have you ever considered Hollywood?"

"They wouldn't be able to handle me out there, and honestly, I don't think I could handle them either."

I considered the steps the police would go through to find me. I knew they'd set up checkpoints around the perimeter, making it even harder for me to escape.

"I need to get out of here, Kenny. Something I've been investigating has gotten too hot, and those involved have killed too many people. But now that they're looking for me, I don't think I'll last long enough to make it to court."

"Jenna, if there's anything I can do . . ."

"You've already done more than you know, Kenny." As I said this, I stepped closer and wrapped my arms around him tightly in a hug.

He gently returned the embrace and murmured, "It's been so long since a beautiful woman hugged me. If this is all I get before I die, I can die happy."

I sniffled as tears blurred my vision.

My pocket vibrated as I received a text from D. It said the cavalry was on its way and to trust them.

"What's going on, Jenna?" Kenny asked.

"Someone I trust told me the cavalry is on its way and that I should do as they say."

Kenny frowned. "How can you believe them?"

He had a point. But then again, Scelisi had inadvertently cleared Kimmel's name by saying she wasn't working with them.

A siren echoed in the distance, getting closer as more uniformed men and women appeared around my house.

The sound of the siren grew louder until an ambulance stopped in front of Kenny's house.

We exchanged glances.

"Looks like this is the calvary."

The EMTs rushed the gurney to the house. Kenny opened the door as I took up a position in the kitchen, gun drawn.

The EMTs barged in and shut the door behind them. Within seconds, guns were aimed at Kenny. One EMT was a large Caucasian man with crew-cut hair, and arms as big as my stomach, and the other was a shorter African American man with a patch over one eye.

"Put your weapons away, or I'll fire!" I shouted.

"Agent Slade? We're here to take you to safety. Who is this man?"

"I'm her security guard and medic. Now lower your guns, or you'll see who I am with my bat."

They holstered their weapons, and I followed suit.

"It's all right, Kenny," I said.

The larger man started, "Mr.—"

"You can call me Kenny."

"Kenny, if you would be willing, it would be helpful if you joined us in case we're stopped. We plan to hide Agent Slade inside the gurney, but having someone on top pretending to look ill may help more."

Kenny was a great help, and he was a kind man. The thought of anything happening to him made my gut ache. I didn't want him to get hurt.

He looked at me, not for permission, but more like to see if I'm worth his risk.

"If Jenna trusts you, then so do I," he said. "Show me what needs to be done."

The EMTs opened the bed like a casket, displaying a very narrow box with air holes.

"Get in, Agent Slade. It won't be comfortable, but we only have a short distance before you can get out."

The second EMT was peering through the windowpane of the door. "Hurry, the cops are coming to the house."

Without hesitation, I hopped into the coffin-like box, and they promptly closed it over me. I'd never had reason to find out if I was claustrophobic. This experience, indeed, tested that. My breath quickened with each passing second as the top of the bed pressed against my nose, making it slightly difficult to even move my hands.

"Police! Open the door."

"Quick, Kenny, lay on the floor," the lead EMT whispered.

The door opened, and the same officer's voice from earlier was back. "What's going on here? I was just here, and the old man seemed fine."

"He dialed 911 and said he was having a heart attack. So, here we are."

I heard footsteps walk around me, but I couldn't see anything.

"It was probably from your harassing me earlier," Kenny wheezed as though he struggled to breathe.

There were motions all around me, and I could see a moment of light through the air holes.

"What are you looking for?" one of the EMTs asked.

"There's a fugitive on the loose and I have orders to inspect everything and everyone."

"Okay, inspect what you want. Just stay out of our way," the lead EMT growled. "One, two, three . . . lift."

Followed by a thud right above me.

"Can you open the door for us, Officer?"

"I'll need to inspect the ambulance before you leave."

"Well, get inspecting. Every second counts."

I'm sure the EMTs tried to be careful wheeling me to the ambulance, but it was far from comfortable in this box. I kept my eyes closed as much as I could. Whenever I opened them, my heart would race, and I needed to remain calm and silent.

"Okay, you're clear to go," the officer said.

The siren blared and the ambulance started moving. A few minutes passed, and I felt a stirring above me before light flooded in. I recoiled at the sudden brightness.

"Who are you?" I questioned the man with the patch sitting on the bench. The larger man was likely driving. Their paramedic uniforms looked genuine, but their overall appearance said they were anything but.

"We're part of a team that specializes in challenging projects."

Kenny sat beside me on the vinyl bench, his expression giving nothing away.

"What is your affiliation with the Bureau?" I asked.

"We were assigned to pick you up. That's all I can tell you. Maybe someone at the safe house will explain further."

"Do you have names?" Kenny asked.

"It's best for all of us that you don't know anything further, so let's just sit tight and enjoy the ride. Okay?"

I'd heard about mercenaries like this, people whom the government called on to take care of things that would otherwise get their hands dirty. This likely fit that category.

We continued for another half hour, but nothing was recognizable outside the window. It gave me time to think about why my father would have gone to such levels of deception. Why not just put everything in either of the secure vaults? How would I have found that key in my desk if not by accident? Would I have gotten another clue, like the bank on the computer? I couldn't help but think someone was guiding me. But if my father was alive, why couldn't he trust me to let me know?

When we came to a stop, the EMT across from me was calm and assuring, as though he knew what was happening. We moved again, and I could see a structure outside of the window. We were inside a building.

Finally, we stopped again.

The EMT said, "This is where you get off. Good luck."

The door swung open as Kenny and I emerged.

Kimmel was waiting in a business suit, and with a smile. We were in the middle of some warehouse. Dusty light spilled through the dirty windows. There was no way to know what color the bricks had been when they were new, or how the sunlight had shone on them before they were covered in grit and grime.

"It's good to see you in one piece, Jenna."

"Where are we?"

"You'll know soon enough. Who's your friend here?" She looked over at Kenny.

"My bodyguard from last night," I replied.

"Morning, ma'am. I'm Kenny, ready to serve again," he said.

Kimmel looked him over with an expression that was almost sad. "Greetings, Kenny," she said. "Do you have any family or friends who could take you in for a few days?"

"My daughter lives in Key Largo, but—"

"Then that settles it. Josh and Fremont, can you two escort Kenny over to his daughter's place, and give them some incentive bonus for the trouble?"

The faux EMTs nodded.

We shared an embrace, then I kissed him on the cheek. "If only I could give you a medal for bravery."

Kenny blushed. "A kiss from a beautiful woman beats a medal any day."

I waved goodbye as he joined Josh and Fremont in a black Mercedes.

"He'll be all right. Follow me," Kimmel said, and walked toward a door.

"Wait, is Fremont the guy with the patch on his eye?"

Kimmel replied, "Yes, he and Josh do side work for us now and then. No worries, your friend will be all right."

The homeless guy had mentioned a man with a patch and a black Mercedes, who had thrown that woman into the dumpster. Didn't the janitor, Freeman, fit the same description?

Did I just put Kenny in danger?

Two banged-up desks and chairs were on either side of some old, recessed metal bookshelves. The air smelled of must, mildew, oil, and machinery.

A dump truck sat between two large doors. The tires were nearly bald, and the truck bed opened. I smiled as a gray cat chased after a mouse behind the truck.

Kimmel walked up to the bookshelves, placed a badge up to a control panel, and a click followed the green light. The bookshelves opened to reveal something that looked like an elevator car, but without buttons or lights.

"Where are we going?" I asked as I followed Kimmel inside.

"You'll see."

I couldn't tell how far down we went, but it was a long, slow descent before the doors opened.

A dimly lit room appeared. It was like a large underground swimming pool with vinyl walls, and long florescent lights hanging from above.

"Hello, Jenna."

"Dad?"

Chapter 26

No words came out. I didn't know whether to cry tears of joy or feel furious.

"I'm sorry, Jenna. I wish there could have been another way."

He was heavier, balder, and his face was fairer than I remembered, but he appeared to be my father.

"Eight years. Eight years, you made me believe you were dead. I looked at your autopsy photographs and cried. How could you—"

"Jenna, we have little time. Is the evidence secure?"

I couldn't believe I was looking at him.

"Agent Slade," Kimmel said, pulling me out of my state of incomprehension.

"I believe so. I hid it . . ."

Wait—I looked around to see we were in a control room. There was an armed female security guard by the elevator door, and one other person staring at a wall of a dozen video screens. One display had footage taken from my house.

"It's okay, Jenna. We're on your side," Kimmel said quickly.

I wanted to ask my father something that only he would know.

"I deposited it with the coin you gave me to keep me safe."

He smiled. "That was a great idea, Jenna. It should be secure there."

He didn't confirm where that location was, nor did he give any hint that he knew what I meant.

"Let's come further inside for a bump of scotch, and I'll explain everything," he said, waving for us to follow him.

We walked farther into what appeared to be a plastic-reinforced cave. "How can we be so far underground in Miami and not be in a swimming pool?"

"Ha, funny you should ask. We're actually next to Homestead Air Force Base. After the hurricane that wiped out the area, this building hardly stood. I bought the property and, using some advanced engineering and polymers, had this underground structure built fifty feet underground. Sure, it leaks occasionally, but no one would ever think I had an underground bunker in Miami."

"How long have you been here?"

My father poured some liquid gold—it was his brand. "After the hurricane destroyed this area in 1992, I realized it would be an ideal place to escape to in the event I needed to. I discreetly hired some contractors from the Middle East, who asked no questions and built this a little at a time."

He sat down, set three glasses on the table, and continued. "I worked for Senator Brandon for a few years, beginning in 2001. He was the most powerful senator in the country, so Scelisi and I didn't think much of providing a favor when he asked."

"What kind of favor?"

"Simple ones at first, like providing armed security for special guests from overseas, then guarding special meetings he would have in remote locations. But then he wanted us more involved in smuggling arms overseas, supporting drug cartels with intelligence— terrible things."

Kimmel nodded while taking a sip of her drink.

"Why did you fake your death?"

"Ah, the million-dollar question . . . I was gathering the evidence of the entire operation, including contact names, dates, and types of weapons going where, when I found out that the CIA was monitoring me. Scelisi learned that a hit had been ordered."

I noted he finished his drink before I had even picked up mine. "Scelisi told me he helped you fake your death. Did you have a relationship with Dr. Jefferies?"

He refilled his glass. "Dr. Jefferies and your mother were the only women I ever bonded with. I wanted to protect her, and was trying to relocate her, but Wilson . . ." He sighed. "Wilson."

"I saw you on a fishing trip with Wilson and Scelisi. Were you friends?"

He looked at Kimmel, who nodded again.

"More like allies of convenience. Wilson got brought on board when Senator Brandon became Vice President Brandon. I never quite trusted him, so I thought I should keep him close. Scelisi realized that what we were doing was so well-protected from above, it never occurred to him not to cooperate."

"Did he know you were compiling the evidence against everyone?"

"No, he didn't. Every now and then, he warned me not to ask so many questions, but he just blew it off."

I swirled my drink in the glass. "I need to better understand after all these years. Why didn't you just take the evidence to someone you trusted?"

He laughed and pointed at me while looking at Kimmel. "That's the instinct of a fabulous investigator."

Kimmel nodded and fought off a cringe. It appeared she didn't have a palate for scotch.

"I had compiled the evidence on a secure hard drive, which I populated every time I went to Switzerland for work. Nearly all of our international arrangements went through Switzerland."

"What about the millions of dollars, and why two vaults?" I asked.

"Another good question." He took a long drink and appeared to put a lot of thought into his answer. "One can never be too safe."

I paused a moment and took a small sip, staring at the table and nodding as though I understood him. Still . . . I wanted to be sure.

"But you would have been better off keeping everything at the hotel. Why did you split the money in both locations?"

"Yeah, you're right. In hindsight, it was possibly over the top."

This was not my father. He looked like him. He was a talented actor. But the money had been located in only one spot.

I maintained my composure. "Ya think? That almost got me killed." I looked around to see where my escapes might be, but there was only the door we came in from, which had an armed guard.

"You have your dad's instinct. Fortunately, Agent Kimmel had your back." He tipped his glass to Kimmel, who did the same back at him.

"I knew what you were going to do there, Jenna," Kimmel added.

"Why didn't you get involved in this investigation?" I asked Kimmel.

"I didn't want to get sucked up into the crime ring. I took advantage of my daughter getting killed, so I could portray myself as someone simply looking to retire."

"Ha, that's how Scelisi described you."

"He's not dead. You wounded him, and he may lose a kidney, but he's going to pull through. I don't think Scelisi would have killed you, but—"

"Well, they sure wanted to wound me, at least," I said, pointing to my arm.

"Jenna, in order to bring down all the big players, I needed more proof. What we had was just some money laundering," the man who was not my father said. "I need the big proof, the proof you got from the facial recognitions and your friend Hamilton, who, by the way, I'm sorry for his loss."

"Wait. You knew about that?"

"Jenna, I've been monitoring you ever since I faked my death. When Scelisi put the surveillance systems in your house, I tapped into them. I've had access to your phone and the burner Kimmel gave you. I've had access to roadside cameras, and anything else I needed to ensure you were safe, and to help guide you."

"Did you send me the picture of that bank?"

He paused and poured more scotch into his glass. "I did. You've impressed me, Jenna. I couldn't be more proud."

"Okay, so, now what? We just live in this hole for the rest of our lives?"

"Kimmel will have everyone leave your house. You can get the evidence, and she'll take you somewhere to turn it in."

I looked at him, then at Kimmel, before glancing around the room, discreetly looking for another exit, and evaluating what the guard was up to. "It's amazing that you could live down here for so many years."

The man acting as my father took a deep breath. "Yes, it's been trying, but we need to hurry, Jenna. Time is of the essence."

"Where will Kimmel take the information?"

"Don't worry about that, Jenna. You'll just have to trust me," Kimmel replied.

I readied my hand to remove my holstered gun. "Where did I hide that evidence, Dad?"

He paused. "You said in a safe place, deposited with the coin I gave you."

I laughed. "It's a good thing we didn't have a dog, or it likely would have dug that buried safe up by now."

Dad also laughed while Kimmel leisurely reached inside her jacket.

I instantly pulled out my sidearm and pointed it at Kimmel just as she pointed hers at me.

"You're pretty smart, Jenna, perhaps smarter than your father," Kimmel said.

"Drop it, and let me go!" I demanded.

The man who portrayed my father said, "Jenna, it's not likely you'll get out of here on your own. So, let's just sit, relax, and talk this out. Many powerful people want that evidence, and will stop at nothing to get it."

"Who the hell are you?"

"I'm your Uncle Jake."

I stared at him. "My Uncle Jake died in prison years ago."

"Dying there would have been easier on me than the twenty years I served. I was a sick man back then and deserved the punishment I received. I wouldn't blame your father for telling you I was dead, but Kimmel arranged for me to be released if I cooperated."

The guard walked up, pointing her rifle at me. "This isn't working. Where is the evidence?"

"Who the hell are you?" I asked.

"That doesn't matter, but everyone here dies if you don't start talking right now."

I remembered from my psychology training that the phrase, "Everyone dies if . . ." is typically one that comes out only in situations where everyone will probably die regardless.

I looked into Kimmel's eyes, but before I could speak, Kimmel fired two rounds at the guard.

The guard was knocked back but got off a round at Kimmel, and another at Uncle Jake, before I shot her in the head.

"Holy shit!" I exclaimed, and jumped back at the cool sensation of blood on my face.

Everything had happened so quickly. The elevator doors were closing with the video-surveillance technician inside.

Kimmel's white blouse had a large circle of red in the center. "Check on Jake."

Jake also had a pool of blood under him, with blood draining from his chest and back.

He looked at me. "Your father did right with you. I'm sorry,

Jenna." It was a death shot through the heart.

He fell limp. I stared at him, never knowing him. My father said he was dead, and then this. A thousand questions raced through my mind, and none of them would be answered.

Kimmel groaned. I quickly grabbed a towel on the counter and placed it against Kimmel's wound—there was a lot of blood.

"Don't worry about me, Jenna," Kimmel said. "You need to get out of here."

"I can't leave you like this." I searched for anything that might help, then asked, "Scelisi said my father was alive. Where is he?"

She coughed up blood. "He lied to you."

"Did you lie to me also?" I asked. "How could you use my uncle like this?"

"He was willing to be expendable if this failed, and if it worked, he'd walk a free man again." Her breathing was raspy, and she coughed up more blood. "When I was in college, I was a part-time bank teller. The bank was robbed, and one of the robbers approached a woman with two children. He put his gun in the woman's hand, pointed it at her children, and told her to decide who would die and who would live. She was terrified, trying to fight him, but he began to count down from ten. The children cried, the mother cried, and I cried. I was helpless."

She coughed up even more blood. I wiped it from her mouth with my jacket.

"When the robber got to one, he forced the mother to pull the trigger and kill her daughter. That horror lived with me my entire life and was the fuel that made me want to join the FBI." She wiped a tear from her cheek. "After my daughter was killed, I tracked down the organization responsible and wanted to kill all of them. They were right here, near Miami. I had everything to go after them, but my leadership denied it."

"Why?"

"I asked myself that question for years. Then I received valuable information that revealed the relationship between that senior agent and the responsible cartel. That agent was getting wealthy for providing protection."

"What organization? Was it the CIA?"

"It was a covert organization that reported directly to the White House. They said they would take care of the problem on one condition. I had to owe them a favor sometime in the future, a favor without question."

"You sold out for revenge?" I asked, shaking my head, wondering how so many senior agents could sell themselves so easily.

She coughed again. "I was furious at the system, and furious that I'd even consider such an offer . . . to give up my oath, and my promise to right the wrongs, and for what? As you said—revenge? That senior agent died in an accident, and the entire cartel responsible for killing my daughter were killed. I thought it would make me feel better, but it didn't . . . at least, not much."

"So, what's this?"

"I was not involved in any of the shit that Scelisi or Wilson were in. I was hoping to retire in a couple of years, but that favor was recently called in, at first to monitor you, but then to get the evidence you've uncovered."

"Who are you working for?"

She stared down at the dead body of Uncle Jake—the body of a man I barely knew, who was killed in cold blood. "Someone senior enough for me to be comfortable doing whatever I need to do to get what she asked for."

"Did you even know my uncle?" I continued.

She shook her head. "I knew your father's brother was on death row for murder and would do anything for a chance to be free. After some makeup, he resembled your father. I just needed to fill in some history, but you were much smarter than anyone gave you credit for. I was told he was expendable, but I wasn't going to kill him."

"What kind of people are you working for? Dark Enterprises? Fuck, Kimmel. What would your daughter think of you now?"

"It's well above Dark Enterprises. You don't understand, Jenna. These people . . . These people will…"

I jumped in. "These people will own you for the rest of your life, and you'll end up like this guy. What word did you use? Expendable? I remember another word you used. Deliverance. Is that what this is?"

"It's not like that, Jenna."

"Tell me, Agent Kimmel, what is it like? Were you going to kill me after I turned over the evidence? Can't have loose ends, you know."

"No, that was not in my orders."

"Not yet. Do you really think they would allow me to live, knowing what I know? I'm a few years older than your daughter would have been. How proud of you do you think she would be right now?" She stared at me, her breath coming out in shallow gasps, and her body trembling. I could tell she had little time left.

"I'll get some help," I said and moved toward the door, but she stopped me with a firm grip on my arm.

"No, Jenna. Those guys upstairs will undoubtedly be waiting for you."

Her gaze shifted away from mine, and suddenly, I realized what had happened.

"You didn't . . . you couldn't have killed Kenny."

"They can't afford to have loose ends. That's what I'm trying to tell you. There are powerful people involved, and they have powerful friends everywhere. My entire job was to get you to bring me to the evidence so I could turn it over and retire with my debt paid while you go on and become the FBI agent you wanted to be. The person who I worked for would have made all of that happen."

"Who is that?"

Kimmel patted my arm and smiled, then winced from the pain. "It's best you don't know."

"Wouldn't I be a loose end?"

She shook her head. "No. I made sure you were not to be harmed."

"I can't believe you stooped to this. I trusted you." I shook my head. We were wasting time. "I need to get you to a doctor. I need to get you out of this mess."

"You already did, Jenna. I can be with my daughter now."

I shook my head frantically, looking around for some other exit, but all I saw was the elevator.

"Is there another way out besides the elevator?"

"There are two air ducts. By now, that surveillance tech must have told Fremont and Josh what happened and they'll likely drop down some agent or explosive to kill us."

I looked around for some clue, something I could use to escape, but I only saw two corpses and Kimmel, who was nodding off.

I grabbed her shoulders and shook her. "You still have a chance to help me escape . . . if you're up for it."

I explained what I planned to do.

She stared into my eyes for a moment before nodding in agreement.

Chapter 27

As the elevator shuddered to a halt, the warehouse floor cast a blinding light that illuminated the sea of twisted corpses pressed upon me as I was sandwiched between them appearing dead with them. I clutched my handgun, just peering out between the two dead bodies, and waited for the inevitable.

"It's her! She's trying to climb into the air duct!" Kimmel shouted as she fumbled with her gun.

Josh snapped to Fremont, "Check it out."

A moment later, a shot rang out, followed by a second, during which I felt Kimmel's body jolt from the strike. My heart almost stopped at the thought of her sacrificing her life to save mine.

"Damn it, Josh! How bad is it?" came a fearful voice.

I then heard an enraged yell, followed by another shot reverberating through the bodies.

"Quick, get the bitch climbing up the vent!" Josh demanded.

The sound of footsteps echoed away until only silence remained.

I sluggishly peeled apart the pile of bodies and saw the larger assailant, Josh, slumped against a post with his hand pressed to a bloody side wound. His eyes widened as he locked with mine, and I pulled the trigger without hesitation, sending him crashing to the ground.

I pushed myself out from under the pile and looked down at Kimmel one last time, mouthing a word of gratitude before sprinting behind a pickup truck about twenty feet away.

"I heard another shot! What happened?" Fremont yelled as he ran back.

An eerie silence followed.

When I peered around the front of the truck, he was nowhere in sight.

Shit.

Frantic now, I stepped behind the truck tire to hide my feet and concentrated on controlling my breathing so I could hear better.

The only sound was my pounding heart. I wanted to believe he left, but my instincts told me he was hunting for me.

I slumped back, desperately hoping the tire would block my view from underneath. My breathing calmed. I peered around the front of the truck again, but still nothing.

Where the hell is he?

The gray cat came from behind some stacked crates, and I felt like I was the mouse it had been chasing earlier.

The cat stopped dead in his tracks and tilted its chin up.

Fremont was on a beam above me.

Without hesitation, I aimed at him and shot. He grabbed hold of the nearest vertical beam without pause and leaped over to another, out of sight.

I shot numerous times, mostly hitting old wood, sending splinters through the air, but it gave me a chance to move to the front of the truck, where he would have the least visibility of me.

"You killed my brother, you bitch! You're not getting out of here alive. You have a choice, Agent Slade. You can end it yourself right now, or if I get you, I'll make sure you suffer a very unpleasant death. Personally, I prefer the latter."

Given they looked very different, they must have been military brothers, which means they were exceptional when it came to tactics to kill people.

"Why didn't you just run me over like you did that poor guy who saw you dumping a body in the dumpster?" I said.

"I do as I'm ordered," he responded. "If you did the same, you may have lived past today."

I peered around the corner of the truck, my heart pounding. A bullet ricocheted off the hood, and I threw myself to the ground. Clambering back to my feet, I frantically sought shelter, but there was nothing close enough to reach without being shot at. He seemed to wait for me to make a move, like that cat waiting outside a mousehole.

Still, if I lifted my head slightly, the truck roof should provide enough cover.

I gradually raised my eyes, and there he was, lined up for a shot. His bullet immediately zinged off the roof. He must have seen the top of my head.

I had no choice now—I had to hunker down and wait him out. If he fell asleep, he'd take a deep drop when gravity got the better of him, but I was at a higher risk of sleeping first with so much blood loss, and exhaustion from two days with little rest.

"Come on, Slade. You can't get away alive. End it on your terms or mine."

I scanned my surroundings, looking for something, or someone, but my only option was to run for a stack of crates in an erratic pattern and hope I didn't get shot. I positioned myself to take off like a sprinter at a track meet, my foot against the truck's bumper, my hands holding me up in a sprinter's stance.

Suddenly, a loud bang echoed from beside the truck, making me jump. I retracted back and peeked around to find a corpse on the ground. I ran to grab it and hit him in the head with it. His exit wound was impressively large. Checking his neck, there was no pulse.

"Jenna? Are you okay?"

Kenny's voice was coming from the open trunk of a black Mercedes.

I ran toward him. "Kenny? What happened? Where were you?"

"After you went into that elevator, they knocked me out cold.

266

When I came to, I was tied up in the trunk of that car. It took some time to get untied, but thankfully, newer cars have an emergency cord inside them, so I eventually got out—and there was this rifle beside me too." He laughed. "Can you believe they kept a gun with me?"

I hugged him again and kissed his cheek. "I owe my life to you, Kenny."

"I told you I'd protect you, Jenna," he said with a smile, glancing over at Agent Kimmel, who was slumped against the elevator doors with two others lying motionless beneath her.

"Thank you." Another tear fell down my face as we both looked around. "I wish I knew what to do next."

"One time, the police tried to fine me for having a dog that bit a postal worker. The only problem was, I didn't have a dog. I took the fine to the police chief, but he wouldn't hear it, so I went to the Channel 10 news outlet. Within twenty-four hours, the fine was ripped up. Maybe you can get to the news?"

At first, I tried to write it off, but then I realized there were so many layers of corruption above me in the Bureau, and the police might be in on it. Everyone I trusted turned out to be against me. It was a good idea.

"Come on, Kenny. Let's get out of here."

We stepped inside the Mercedes and drove away.

There was one news anchor with the most extensive following in the country. If anyone could expose this while keeping me alive, it was him.

I desperately needed to change my clothes. Between sweat and blood, I was a walking murder scene. I couldn't get caught on a security camera, so Kenny was a dear and walked into the department store to get a size-six pantsuit and blouse. I instructed him to find something he would get for his daughter.

He returned, and I went into the back seat to change.

"You know, I've never bought any clothes for my daughter before," Kenny admitted.

"No? Why not?"

"My wife always did that with her, and when she passed away, my daughter was too old for me to buy clothing for her. I always thought about doing it for my granddaughter, but . . . I don't know. Wouldn't that be a little weird?"

I remembered back when I was perhaps seven, and my father took me clothes shopping. His eyes lit up with every outfit I tried on. When I'd ask which one he liked most, he said all of them."

"I'm sorry. Maybe take your daughter and granddaughter out, and make a day of it . . . for both of them?"

He nodded as I put on my shoes and got back into the driver's seat.

When we pulled up to the front of the news building in downtown Miami, two armed security officers stood guard at the entrance.

"Kenny, can you wait here? If they try to ticket the car, just drive it around the block a few times until I come out."

"That sounds good, but I haven't had a driver's license for the past fifteen years."

"It's okay. I'll be right back."

"Ma'am, can I help you?" the front clerk asked.

"I'm Agent Slade. I need to meet with Sean Murphy. It's urgent."

"Yes, ma'am. He's not at this location, but I'll call and see if he's available."

She began to make a call while I looked around the glamorous facility. Video monitors filled many parts of the building, and there appeared to be multiple desk areas. I thought they did their news from one location and just changed the background appearance.

"Ma'am." She handed me the phone.

"Hello, Agent Slade, this is Sean Murphy. How can I help you?"

I paused for a few seconds, recalling what I went through over the past week, the people I'd killed and who had tried to kill me, the FBI involvement, my father being alive and then not alive, and Kenny to the rescue.

"Agent Slade?"

"Yes. I've just been through hell over the past week, dealing with corruption and murder at levels of leadership I don't feel safe discussing over the phone. I'm taking a risk that this phone is being monitored, but if you get down here to Miami in the next twenty-four hours, I'll have a story of all stories for you. One that exposes the largest corruption ring the world has ever seen."

"Can you give me anything more than that?" Murphy asked.

"I can't over the phone, but I assure you, it will uncover corruption and levels beyond comprehension."

"I'll be there as soon as I can. How do I contact you?"

"I'll contact you."

I returned the phone to the clerk. "Thanks."

Outside, the Mercedes was missing. There was no sign of Kenny.

"Do you know where my car went?" I asked the security officers.

"A couple of your bureau guys pulled up and drove off in the car."

I scanned the area, furious at how quickly they'd found me. Were they tracking me somehow, or maybe tracked my name through the phone call? Were they using illegal surveillance?

A man in a typical FBI black suit and black tie and no emotion walked up. "Agent Slade. You need to come with me."

"Who are you?"

He pulled out an FBI badge. "I'm Agent Hackney. I think it's best we not make a scene here."

"Why don't you Feds take your sandbox games somewhere else?" one guard said.

Hackney turned to him. "You can either shut your mouth and forget you ever saw us here, or I'll have your ass in Guantanamo within an hour, just because I can."

I considered running away, but Kenny was in their clutches. Then again, he'd proven to be quite resourceful.

If I didn't go with him, I'd have many more agents surrounding the area within minutes. If I did, I risked getting myself killed.

"Trust me, Agent Slade, I'm not with the bad guys."

I snapped a disbelieving gaze into his eyes. "Do you know how many people told me that and then tried to kill me in the past forty-eight hours?"

"We know about Kimmel. If you had stayed there, we could have found you and helped. Come on, let's meet up with your friend."

"If you're on my side, why would you take him away?"

His grip on my arm surprised me. "I'm done messing around. Come with me."

I yanked the gun out of my holster and pointed it straight at Agent Hackney. "You won't lay a hand on me," I spat.

The security guards reacted instantly, their guns coming up in perfect synchronization. "Guns drawn, get Miami PD here straight away!" one of them barked into his transmitter.

Hackney sneered. "Tsk, tsk, you shouldn't have done that," he hissed before turning tail and walking away.

I lowered my weapon as he disappeared around the corner. My momentary relief was cut short by a deep command from behind me. "Drop the gun! Now!"

Holding my hands in plain sight, I calmly replied, "Based on what happened here, who do you think is in the wrong? I'm going to slowly holster my gun." I deliberately holstered it without incident.

The guard growled. "Let's wait for the cops to sort it out. Raise your hands!"

I raised my hands again. "I am not a threat to you. I'm on my way to find my friend they just kidnapped."

The first police car screeched to a halt, two officers leaping out with guns already leveled at me. "Drop your gun! Now!"

"I'm an FBI agent. I will slowly open my jacket to show you my badge." At a snail's pace, I opened my jacket, exposing my badge on my belt. The security guards nodded to each other in understanding, promptly holstering their weapons as the police lowered theirs. Two more cars pulled up in a dazzling show of bright blue lights.

Finally, an unmarked car arrived.

Detective Rodriguez approached me. "Hello, Agent Slade. It appears our paths cross again."

I nodded. "It would appear so."

"I'd like you to come back to the station and answer a few questions."

"Well, I have a lot of answers for you, but going back to the station would be a death trap, as I've nearly been killed by several of my own recently. And they took my friend."

He nodded. "I understand. I don't think they'll do anything with your friend. Let's take a ride and think this through."

"Why would I take a ride with you?"

"Because I went to the police academy with your father, and it doesn't look like you have another ride."

My lips tightened, tempted to call him out.

He waved off the other officers, who returned to their cars and drove off.

"It's true," said Rodriguez. "I told Charlie all about Miami, and he got assigned down here when he graduated. We became friends while on the Miami police force, but he joined the FBI. He said that was where the action was, while I wanted to make a difference in my home city. After he met Scelisi, we didn't talk much. I heard about his passing, but I couldn't believe it. He loved you way too much to have done that to himself. I tried to look into it, but the FBI adamantly told me to leave it alone. Sadly, I complied."

"Why have I never heard of you?"

"We had a falling out when he told me some of the things he was doing. I was shocked that he would do such things. You were probably five or six years old then."

Part of me wanted to believe him. He seemed familiar. "Okay. He has some old pictures on his wall at the house. If I see you in those pictures, I'll believe you."

"Then let's go."

Until recently, I'd always taken pride in my ability to judge people's character. Rodriguez didn't appear to be forceful or insincere. Besides, if I were to find Kenny, I'd need some type of insider to help me.

When we arrived at my house, a marked police car was parked in front.

"Stop here. Everyone is undoubtedly watching for us, so I'll hide while you talk to them and ask them to leave for an hour or two."

He nodded.

As he drove into the driveway, I curled up as small as possible in the passenger seat. Rodriguez stepped out, the door shut, and I heard a distant conversation. Then he returned and said through the window, "It's all clear now."

I cautiously exited the car, looking around for any sign of FBI or police cars.

Nothing.

"Come on," I said.

The front door was unlocked. Everything inside was in tatters, my furniture smashed and drawers overturned. My kitchen had been ransacked, and the freezer door had been left open. My ice cream collection was ruined, and a pool of water was on the floor.

Down the hallway, Dad's office had also suffered severe destruction. And there, on the ground where I'd last seen Porter, lay a pool of dried blood.

"I'm sorry, Jenna," Rodriguez said, offering his sympathies as I stared at the carnage.

"His pictures are in the broken glass on the table over there," I said. "I need to use the restroom. Look for a photo of you with him."

Upstairs, in my bedroom, the mattress was ripped open, stuffing everywhere. But my secret panel was untouched, and that was when it hit me—I had put my lucky coin in my pocket moments before Scelisi knocked on the door. With relief, I pulled it out and looked at the bronze picture, caressing the imprint of my father.

Are you alive?

The wall opened up to reveal everything I'd placed inside. A wave of relief washed over me as I ran to my bedroom, grabbed my empty backpack, and then returned to place everything inside.

I thought about all those who had died just for this hidden information. Then I chucked some sleepwear and a few other clothes inside the backpack, making sure not to strain its zipper too much. After that, I returned to my father's office to find Rodriguez studying photographs.

"What did you find?"

He showed me one of him standing next to my father at the police academy. "This was our graduation picture." He handed another one to me. "Here is one of us at Cliffy's Bar. It's closed now, but it was a place we went to often."

There was certainly a resemblance between him and the younger man in the picture, but what really convinced me was seeing his eyes beginning to water. That was all the proof I needed.

"Keep in mind, this was like forty years ago. I've gained a wrinkle or two, and a little more weight."

"Okay, I believe you . . . for now."

"Did the Bureau do this to your house? And whose blood is that?" He pointed to where Porter had fallen.

"Agent Scelisi came in and tried to force me to do something. I refused and was shot in the arm in the living room. I ran back here, and another agent shot at me through that window. I hid, and when he climbed through, I shot him over there."

"Jesus, what do they want from you?"

I looked at my smashed computer and copier. At my father's destroyed desk.

"Evidence of one of the largest corruption rings this world has ever seen."

I looked around the room, remembering my entire life in this house. If I made it out of this alive, maybe it was time to sell it and get something smaller.

"Those officers won't be gone long," he said. "We should probably get going."

"Didn't you want to interrogate me? I thought you had questions."

"You've answered them. Is the evidence your father had in that backpack?"

"Inspector, I'm just beginning to trust you, but I'll shoot anyone who interferes with me at this point."

He backed off and held up his hands. "I'm not getting in your way. Just tell me how I can help."

"Do you know a safe place for me to spend the night?"

Chapter 28

An apartment over Yao Ming's Diner was the last place I expected to hide for the night. Inspector Rodriguez had undoubtedly come through for me. But this place? And across from Dark Enterprises? Irony was an understatement.

"I am grateful for you finding me a safe spot, but . . ."

The inspector smiled. "Maybe the Marriott would be better? No security cameras here."

"Do you pay for this apartment with police department funds?"

"In a way. I use money taken during raids and create some special categories in our accounting reports to cover it. Should be secure."

"I do appreciate your helping me, but I have a question."

"Go ahead."

"Scelisi told me my father was alive. Something about a drug he gave him. Do you know anything about that?"

He laughed and shook his head. "That guy could pull off some crazy shit, but when I attended his funeral, I hadn't seen him for years. And even then, only from a distance."

"I don't remember seeing you there."

"There were a lot of FBI there who I didn't respect very much, so I was in my car. He was a wonderful friend." He walked to the door to the apartment and opened it. "Good night, Jenna. Tomorrow is a new day." Then he closed the door.

After locking it behind him, I turned to assess my room for the night. The rank scent of burned cooking oil and incense was everywhere. Still, it had a pull-out bed, and no one would likely know I was there.

I dropped my backpack onto a wooden chair beside a wobbly table, its uneven legs propped up with folded paper. The apartment had sparse furnishings: a two-burner stove, a couple of cabinets, and a bathroom that was as small as most airplane bathrooms, an armchair next to the dark-green sleeper sofa from the seventies, and a coffee table that was in desperate need of refinishing.

After taking a deep breath, I headed for a much-needed shower, thankful for my sleek physique as I fumbled with the handheld showerhead.

A week ago, I'd complained about my old car. Now I was wanted by every law enforcement agency in the country. But for one night, at least, I tried not to think about it as I crawled into bed, counting the springs beneath me and listening for any sound that might be trouble.

A distant gunshot made my eyes snap open.

The light from the streetlamp peeking through the window was enough to make out the shadows of my surroundings. Everything appeared to be good, nothing threatening or out of place. But with my heart thundering like a freight train, I knew that going back to sleep anytime soon was impossible.

I groggily checked my watch—4:00 a.m., one of the worst times at night to wake up. By the time I got back to sleep, I'd need to wake up soon after. It felt like everything was against me.

Feeling thirsty, I stumbled toward the kitchen sink and opened a cabinet in search of a glass. To my horror, two small roaches scurried along the door as if it were their own personal racetrack. Disgusted, I held up the glass to the glow of the streetlamp to check if it was clean. Thankfully, it was at least washed—water streaks glistened on its surface. When I turned on the tap, rusty brown water poured out instead of clear liquid.

I hesitated as I contemplated whether to actually drink this grimy water, torn between knowing it was only iron and fear of what else could lurk in that line. Deciding against it, I set the glass back in the cabinet.

I sank into a battered armchair beside a small coffee table and gazed out the window, wondering when I had last experienced a peaceful and ordinary day. All I had wanted was my first murder case. But my boss had set me up, and after days of relentlessly investigating and uncovering dark secrets, I felt more uncertain than ever about what was happening.

My mind kept coming back to that Senior Agent Hackney, who had approached me at the news station. He knew about Kimmel, yet I couldn't remember having seen him before. He seemed to know an awful lot about what had happened in that secret location. And how did he know I was at the news studio?

With trembling hands, I opened Hamilton's envelope, attempting to read by the dim light, hoping for some answers. Inside were details of trust funds being funneled into the accounts of numerous people and companies, paying out millions to Brandon, Dark Enterprises, Scelisi, Wilson, and many others.

One other name stood out: Donte was paid handsomely a couple of times.

I thought back to that night, thankful he hadn't taken advantage of me.

Was this all bribe money? For what, though? For streamlining the logistics, brokering illegal activities, smuggling weapons?

Upon these women's deaths, whoever held the trust would distribute the money to all its beneficiaries. But who, exactly, was the trustee on these accounts? If I were to bet, the trustee was Dark Enterprises. The only way I'd get that knowledge was at their headquarters, and likely in one of those rooms I didn't have access to.

Wait, wasn't there a law firm on the lower floors of that building? Damn, what was their name? But then again, it could be another front. Last time I'd investigated, I'd been knocked out and awoke to find Sueann dead in my bed. I bet all the paperwork associated with those trust funds and bank accounts were in those locked classified rooms. I'd need a search warrant to access them. I wanted to do more research on the law firm there. No longer having a laptop or cell phone really sucked.

As soon as I disclose everything to Sean Murphy, he'll blow the lid off this mess.

Chapter 29

Instincts had me pointing my gun toward the sound of clanking metal outside.

"Jenna, it's me . . . Rodriguez."

I blinked the sleep from my eyes, set my gun, and unlocked the door to let him in.

"Not how I like my mornings to start, with a gun pointed at me, but under the circumstances, I'm glad you didn't shoot me. I'd hate to think that someone would waste this sausage, egg biscuit, and coffee," said Rodriguez.

"The day's still early, and thank you. I'm starving." I tore into the bag and bit into a biscuit of bliss.

"If you were looking to turn over your evidence to a certain news anchor, I'll let you know now that the entire media station is covered with secret agents from all over the state. Also, a certain Sean Murphy has an FBI detail monitoring his every move."

285

I fell back on the bed, holding my sandwich. "I'm so fucked! It's just a matter of time before I'm dead. Go ahead and do it, get a promotion in, it's going to happen anyhow."

"Jenna, I'm not going to shoot you, but I will help you. My wife of thirty years was killed by the same cartel that killed Agent Kimmel's daughter, and I couldn't do a thing about it. A person came to me as they did Kimmel, but I didn't want to owe anyone. That's how it always plays out. If you take a deal once, it will haunt you forever."

"You knew about Kimmel's daughter?"

"I've been with this police force for a long time, and not much happens without my knowing about it. We talked at Cliffy's once about what she could do. I advised her not to get involved, but she had vengeance in her blood."

I sat up. "So, what do I do now?"

"Well, the word on the street is that there's an order to shoot you on sight," he said.

"Wait, something like that exists?" I asked.

"Not officially—but the FBI put out a million-dollar reward for bringing you in, dead or alive, and someone will be after that money any second now."

"So, either get shot or get shot—great!" I replied sarcastically, "Just do it now, collect the money, and retire a happy man."

He chuckled. "Jenna, again . . . I will not shoot you, nor will I bring you in. I suspect every electronic device within a few hundred miles has your name on it, and every video camera is searching for your face."

My tone was somber. "I don't know what to do without advice from someone I trust."

"You have one of the greatest gifts your father could have given you," he said gently. "Use your instincts. They've kept you alive to this point."

"Inspector . . . "

"Please, call me Juan."

"Okay, Juan. Do you have a laptop in your car, by chance?"

"I do, why?"

I pulled the hard drive and other devices from my backpack. "Why not see if we can't figure this out?"

"I have IT security on my laptop too, you know."

"Turn off the Wi-Fi. If this is what I think it is, you will be able to easily defend the use of it."

He ran downstairs as I pulled out my coin again. *Dad, give me some guidance.*

Juan returned to the abbreviation of an apartment and set his laptop on the wooden table.

"I'd like to borrow your phone while you're booting that up."

He handed it to me and watched as I took a toothpick found in the kitchen drawer and opened the small port on the side.

"Don't ruin my phone," he said. "I just got this one."

"It's all good. I want to see what people died for on this SIM card I got from Dr. Jefferies's office."

"It seems quite a few people are dying around you." When I looked up, his expression told me he wished he could take it back. "I'm sorry. That wasn't right of me."

I inserted Dr. Jefferies's chip and pulled up the files. They were all here. The Jane Does' toxicology reports, their names, and the report on the man killed who'd worked at Dark Enterprises. I searched for one more report, but after scanning everything, I couldn't find it.

"Is everything okay?" Juan asked.

"Yeah, I was just hoping . . . never mind."

"The laptop is ready to go. Now, if you'll please put my phone back together, I'd appreciate it."

I fumbled to replace his original phone chip and handed it back to him, then plugged in the hard drive I got from the hotel. Juan clicked on the program file, bringing up the same screen Justin had found at the hotel in Switzerland, requiring a long password.

"Here is the impasse. A 256-character code. How would anyone remember this?"

"We use a sixteen-bit passcode on our computers. I usually use a song or a rhyme I can remember."

"A rhyme? Oh, my God! Wait—"

I pulled out the thumb drive with the family pictures and the identification of the women who were killed.

"There's a favorite nursery rhyme on there my father saved. Bring it up."

He brought up the file "Remember." The nursery rhyme was "Hickory Dickory Dock."

"Copy and paste that into the password entry."

It couldn't be that simple. All of this super-secret-vaulted-spy shit, and the password was on a thumb drive in my bedroom all this time? Why wouldn't the FBI have taken it when they took everything else?

The small hourglass spun in a circle in the middle of the screen.

Invalid Password.

I kicked the leg of the pull-out sofa. "I could have sworn that was it. I was never so confident about anything in my entire life." I walked to the kitchen, combing my hands through my hair. "Can we count the characters in that nursery rhyme?"

Juan clicked on a few buttons and saw it was 244.

"Ugh, I thought for sure that was it," I said, placing my hand on my forehead, trying to think.

Juan asked, "Do these O's look like zeros?"

"That's odd." I looked at the spacing of the rhyme, the letters, and numbers. "Wait, characters are also required in a passcode with letters and numbers, right? Place periods after each part."

Juan placed a period after each one while I tapped the top of the chair with my fingernails. He checked the character count, and we both looked at the 256 and turned to each other in astonishment.

Juan copied and pasted into the password space and pressed enter. The same spinning hourglass spun around again.

A screen came up, as did another. Many pages layered onto the computer monitor and kept on loading. Hundreds of pages . . . it seemed like it would never stop.

I jumped up and yelled out, "Oh my God! It worked!"

Juan was about to touch a computer key when I said, "Wait for it to stop on its own."

The minute of waiting seemed like an eternity, but it finally stopped.

Juan scanned down on the top file and saw an invoice for bolts.

"This is nothing but an invoice for hardware." He paged through the next one and saw the same with nuts, another for screws, another for lumber, then farming tools. "This is worthless information."

"What if I told you each item was a code word for weapons? Look at the costs for that hardware."

A square of shingles was a $100,000.

"That can't be right," he said.

"It can if those shingles were a crate of military rifles."

"How would you prove it?"

"That is, perhaps, the only missing piece to the entire case. We could try to get a crate I hid down at the docks, but it's guarded, and I'd want to avoid security as much as possible. There's only one person alive who can almost certainly help us, but it might take some influence."

Juan laughed to himself.

"What's so funny?"

"You sound a lot like your father."

I leaned down and hugged him. "Thank you. Thank you for trusting me."

"I regret I didn't fight to keep your father out of trouble. He was a good man. Now, does my phone work or did you break it?"

Chapter 30

A police car was parked in front of Scelisi's house.

"Apparently, they're wise to you already," Juan said.

We drove around the block to find his yard fenced.

"How are you at climbing fences?" he asked.

"I'm not sure I can do it with one arm, but if I get a boost . . ."

I was reluctant to leave the backpack, but for now, it might be safe in the trunk of a police investigator.

We walked up to the fence surrounding Scelisi's yard and peeked through the panels. Security cameras pointed in multiple directions.

"There's no getting through that yard without being seen," Juan said.

"What do you suggest?"

He thought for a moment. "Wait here. I'll drive around, have the uniformed officers go off on a task, and watch for them. Scelisi likely has a front door camera as well."

"Okay, how do we get to him?"

"You hug the wall and stay in the bushes. I'll knock on his door, and hopefully, he opens it for me. I'll ask him how he's doing, and that's when I'll push him inside and disarm him. You follow behind me and close the door."

"That's a tremendous risk for you. You could be fired . . . or worse."

"From what I saw on those files, the bigger crime would be for me to do nothing."

I placed my hand on his shoulder. "I wish my dad had stayed friends with you."

"I may just be with him soon enough if this goes sideways," he said. He didn't wait for me to respond before walking to his car.

After creeping around Scelisi's house, I hid behind the bushes just as Juan had suggested. The police car was fifty feet in front of me. If they really paid attention, they might see me, but I moved slowly so I wouldn't catch their eye.

Juan pulled up behind the squad car, stepped out, and walked to the driver-side He laughed a bit with them, and then, after a brief discussion, they waved and drove off.

Juan didn't even look my way as he rang the bell.

"Yes. Who is it?" Scelisi's voice came through the speaker.

"I'm Inspector Rodriguez from Miami PD. I have a few questions about Agent Jenna Slade."

"What kind of questions?"

"The kind of questions that you might not want to discuss too loudly outside and over this device."

"Let me see your badge."

Juan held his badge in front of the camera.

"Okay, give me a few minutes."

He was likely calling in to verify who Juan was.

Two minutes later, he said, "I'll be right down. Step down to the first stair, away from the door."

Damn. Scelisi was good. I was never taught that.

Juan followed his directions, and the door opened. I could see Scelisi in the door's crack, and then I saw the metal of a gun in his hand. Juan would not see that from his angle.

"What's your question?" Scelisi barked.

Rodriguez furrowed his eyebrows. "Really? You want me to ask you like this? I could just take you downtown, since the questions are of national importance."

Scelisi challenged, "If they were that important, then why isn't the FBI asking me?"

Damn, another good question. Juan needed to up his game.

"It's about the murder of Agent Charlie Slade, Jenna's father, and her accusation that you murdered him."

"That bitch is lying. I told her he was alive."

"Is he? I thought he was buried. Do you really want to have this discussion like this?" Juan waved his hands at the door.

Scelisi opened the door a little more and peeked around to the other side to ensure no one was lurking. "Where's the marked cruiser that was out here?"

"I don't know. Maybe they went to get some doughnuts."

Scelisi muttered, "I don't like this," he whispered.

Faster than I could blink, Juan slammed into the front door. The sound of a gunshot went off as they both fell into the house.

I hurried onto the porch, stepped inside, and swiftly closed the door to find Juan in a scuffle with Scelisi and his firearm. I whipped out my weapon and strode around to where Scelisi could see me.

"Drop it now," I ordered.

He stopped, stared at me, and complied. After Juan freed himself, I saw that the bandage on Scelisi's side was stained red with blood.

"Nice move, Jenna," said Scelisi. "You managed to catch me off guard. So, what now?"

"Seeing as you're the only one alive aware of certain secrets, I don't think your services will be necessary for long," I said.

He chuckled. "Jenna, these are the kind of people who make the Pope disappear. You might want to use what few days you have left wisely. Maybe you have an extra day with the help of your cop buddy here."

"I just need something before we part ways: one of those packages you've been helping smuggle overseas that contains bolts, or nuts, or whatever."

He laughed again. "What do you know about that?"

"We know a great deal about it now," Juan said. "In fact, your name is on some paperwork showing the delivery of goods from a trust."

"You've got nothing on me."

I knelt beside him. "We have everything on you and everyone involved worldwide. It can go quite smoothly for you if you just get me a crate."

"We'd never get close to a crate. We would both get killed before we got to one."

"If we don't, we're dead already," I said. "So, why not try to die doing something good for once? Something tells me you're the one who convinced my father to get involved in all this to begin with."

He stared at me as though trying to remember back in time. "Okay, I'll try to help you get a crate, but then I want some of that cash your father has. And I want to slip away on a ship, never to be seen again."

"You get me that crate, and I can't care less where you go. And you can have all that cash. It only makes people greedier, and that's the last thing I want in my life."

"We can take my car," Juan offered.

"Do you even know where to go?" Scelisi said.

"The docks," I said.

Chapter 31

"You won't find what you're looking for down here," Scelisi said as we approached the guard shack.

"For your sake, I hope we do."

"Why would you even say that? It's not like you'll kill me. You're too good for that."

"Really? How did you get that wound on your side?"

"That was an impulse reaction. You couldn't kill me in cold blood."

He was right. I didn't have it in me to kill anyone in cold blood, but I needed to get a particular crate I'd hidden, which meant that I might do more than I usually would to get it.

After we drove down to the water, a dock worker with a white hat stopped us. Juan rolled down his window as the man approached.

"This is your time to shine and right the wrongs you've done," I whispered to Scelisi.

"This is a restricted area. Let me see some identification," the worker bellowed. His accent was more New England than Miami.

"I'm Inspector Rodriguez from the Miami PD. We're investigating a murder, and I'm with someone who may be authorized to be here."

The back window rolled down.

"Oh, Agent Scelisi. Are you all right?"

"Yeah, Frank, I'm fine. I was wounded the other day, but I need to check on something from a recent shipment.

"Damn. I hope you got the bastard."

"He sure did," I said. "Won't be snooping around anymore from six feet under."

Frank laughed. "That's what I'm talking about. Yeah, you're good. Hope you're better soon."

Scelisi waved. "Thanks, Frank."

Juan drove another twenty feet to the entrance.

"I'm telling you, you won't find anything here," Scelisi said.

"Juan, do you have a flashlight? I seem to be missing mine."

"Always right here," he replied, pulling it out of his jacket pocket.

We all stepped out of the car. Juan helped Scelisi exit, then followed me to the door. I opened it, and Juan turned on his flashlight.

Not much had changed except for more dust particles floating in the air.

"This way," I said, pushing Scelisi forward.

We walked to where I had stashed the crate. Thankfully, it was still there beneath its cardboard.

"Quick, shine your light on the table over there."

Juan did while I went to get the small pry bar. I walked back to the crate and pried off the lid. A bunch of nuts rested in the crate, just as I'd left them.

"Where did you get this?"

"I sneaked in here before they took everything away," I replied.

"Why did you even need me?" Scelisi said. "You could have come down here on your own."

"I needed you as assurance so the security wouldn't get in the way."

"Okay, then, you've got your crate. Now let me get on my way. I don't want to be with you when someone finds out you have this."

"Shut up, Scelisi. Jeez, no wonder my father decided to investigate this crime network. He almost certainly couldn't take any more of you."

I pushed the nuts as far to one side as possible and pried at the edge of the false bottom. A chunk of wood popped out, then another, and another. I reached into the small hole and found what I was looking for.

I held up a small-arms bullet.

Juan whispered, "Damn!"

"We're all dead. You know that, right?" Scelisi touted. "Now what? Who do you trust to bring all this evidence to? This is far bigger than you could possibly imagine."

Juan added, "He's possibly right. Your face and name are pretty hot right now."

"What do you suggest?"

After a long pause, Juan asked, "Do you still have my back on that retirement package?"

I laughed. "Absolutely."

"Good. You know all the bigwigs are coming to Dark's headquarters for a big conference, right?"

"Yeah."

"We've been tasked to provide security for the FBI Deputy Director while she's here. I can get you in front of her, and you can present everything you have."

"Is she in on it too?" I asked Scelisi.

"I don't know who's above Hackney. It's undoubtedly better that way."

Hackney was the agent who had tried to take me at the news station, the agent who'd taken Kenny.

"I remember him. Do you know where he took my friend Kenny?"

"Who knows, maybe he's buried somewhere by now."

I punched him in his wound. I wouldn't normally do such a

thing, but now I was getting pissed.

Scelisi buckled over and moaned, "I don't know who Kenny is."

"Okay, I believe you, just stop pissing me off."

"Jenna, the longer you keep this evidence to yourself, the more you risk it never getting to the right people," Juan said.

I studied the situation, looked down at the crate of stainless-steel nuts.

"I like your idea, Juan, but with one little modification."

Chapter 32

"No matter how often I'm in small places like this, I never get used to it," I said from the hidden compartment in Juan's car.

"How many times have you been confined in places like that?"

"Lately, more than I care to admit. People who have these types of compartments are usually up to no good."

Juan laughed. "Was that a question?"

"How much farther until we get there?"

"We have one more checkpoint, and then we'll be at the back loading entrance to Dark Enterprises. Just take deep breaths and close your eyes. It'll help."

"I learned that technique last time."

"I have that compartment to store my riot gear, extra weapons, and other things I don't want to be found if someone breaks into my car. And it's small enough to where no one will easily notice it."

"At least turn on the air-conditioning."

The car stopped, and I heard a voice. "What are you doing back here?"

"I'm Inspector Rodriguez from Miami PD. I'm assisting with security for the conference."

There was a pause. I pondered leaving Scelisi tied up at that apartment above Ming's, and even more so having Juan help me, but there was no way we could have him warning anyone. Keeping all the evidence there was the larger risk, but Juan assured me that no one would have a reason to go to that apartment. There was too much at stake, and my entire life relied on everything going right.

"Can you open your trunk?"

"Really? I'm a police officer."

"Just open the trunk."

Partial daylight invaded the liner of the hidden compartment as the trunk opened.

"Okay, you're good to go."

"Just as advertised," Juan boasted a few minutes later.

I said, "Great, now we just need to get me in front of the Deputy Director with a hundred agents and officers there to ensure no one gets near her."

"Leave that to me," Juan said.

"Why are you certain you can get me in front of her?"

"I'm just sure of it."

The car stopped again.

"We have another issue," Juan said. "We're at the back entrance of the building, but there are two security cameras that will definitely spot you getting out of the trunk. Wait, I've got a strategy. I will open the trunk. You hold the string hanging on the trunk door to keep it from opening too much, and when the camera is blocked, run for that part of the building, stay along the wall, and scoot underneath into the building."

I pushed the false wall, rolled out of the hidden compartment, and grabbed onto the pull string. "Got it."

A sliver of light followed the metallic click under the trunk door, but I held it open just enough to peek through.

Holding tight to the pull string inside, I made sure not to let it close as Juan reached up to one of the warehouse workers, something in his palm. The forklift driver glanced around before tucking whatever it was away in his pocket.

The driver returned with a tall stack of crates and set it down directly in front of the camera above Juan—genius! Then he drove away again. When it was safe, I opened the trunk door carefully, stepped out, closed it quietly, and stayed low, under the security camera's line of sight, until I stood beside Juan.

"I guess you've done this kind of thing before?" I asked as we hastily walked through the warehouse.

"A few times, yeah. A lot of these people aren't getting paid what they deserve."

After Juan and I made our way through the warehouse, he checked that it was safe for me to enter the hallway beyond.

"Wait here for a minute, okay?" he said, disappearing through the door.

He was gone before I could ask if I had a choice.

As time ticked on, I started to worry what would happen if he got caught or thrown out. I was planning my escape when the door opened again: Juan.

"I had to pay one of the servers a month's worth of salary to take the day off and let me borrow her uniform—here."

He handed me the outfit I'd seen the servers wearing at the last gala.

I asked him to turn around while I changed. "This isn't the kind of risk most people take right before retirement. Why?"

"I told you already. I wanted to retire alongside my wife, visiting every continent on our bucket list." He chuckled. "The detail she put into the itinerary always irritated me. After her death, it took weeks before I could think straight again. I know she would want me to help you, and so would your father—no matter what some of his decisions were, he was still a good friend."

"There! All done."

He looked over to see me dressed to serve. The buttons on the white blouse seemed to test the integrity of the sewing, but the gold vest covered most of it.

"Ready?" he asked.

"I am, providing these buttons hold out."

Juan and I hurriedly made our way through the hallway until we encountered a man with an earpiece and suit. "Excuse me, can you help? I found her taking a wrong turn and trying to find the kitchen, where she works. Is there any way we could help her?"

The security guard eyed us both before he asked for identification. Juan handed him his badge, and then the officer looked at me. "Miss, do you have your ID with you?"

I pretended to freeze in embarrassment. "I'm sorry, it's my first day here, and I'm so nervous I left it in the car. I really need this job. Please let me go."

He muttered something into his sleeve that a woman in a server's uniform was lost. I smiled nervously while rocking from heel to toe, hoping he would think I was a simple girl, scared and embarrassed.

"Okay, they've been looking for you. The kitchen is through those doors and to the left."

We moved in the pointed direction before Juan said to me quietly, "Come out here frequently, and look for me and the Deputy Director. If I make eye contact with you, make your way to us."

I nodded. "Good luck."

"You too."

I walked into the kitchen, feeling a sense of foreboding as an angry voice yelled from across the room. "Where the hell have you been? Did you do something with your hair? You look different. We have a thousand guests, and every server counts. Now take that tray of hors d'oeuvres out and smile."

I grabbed the tray, trying to avoid anyone's gaze. The kitchen manager didn't even recognize his staff other than a pretty face and long hair.

Even though I recognized several people, none of them seemed to recognize me. As I made my way around the room, I tried to make myself invisible by saying, "Hors d'oeuvres?" calmly and averting my eyes.

When I returned to the kitchen, Sarah Hanvey-Dark was talking to the chef. I didn't want her to see me, so I spun on my heel and veered toward the restroom.

Peering under all the stall doors, I was relieved to find they were empty. Looking into the mirror, I said with determination: "You've got this, Jenna."

I inhaled a deep breath, thinking I should have learned how to meditate. Then I stepped back into the ballroom, frantically scanning for signs of Sarah's presence. She was gone.

"Where have you been? You must be faster!" a petite Italian man bellowed, pushing me toward another steaming tray of grilled lamb chops. "Hurry out there and serve!"

Serving staff walked in and out of the kitchen. It was challenging to walk around the many suits in the crowd, hoping to not round one person and bump into someone who would recognize me. I hastened through the crowd as chatting guests plucked lamb chops from my tray, urgently searching for Juan, but he was nowhere to be seen.

Once the platter was empty, I spun around to return to the kitchen but bumped into someone, dropping the platter to the floor. I looked up to see Trevor Dark.

"Jenna! It is you! How kind of you to join us," Trevor Dark boomed in a deafening tone that silenced the chatter instantly. A dozen guns surrounded me before I could even attempt to form a response.

Sarah stepped forward, her stony gaze piercing directly into my soul. "You must be a complete idiot to show up here after killing one of our own men and so many FBI agents."

"What's happening here?" A woman in a suit barged through the barricade of security personnel. "Who is this?"

Agent Hackney strode up beside her and declared, "This is the FBI agent who eliminated our finest agents in Miami, and who has been on the lam. Put cuffs on her and take her into custody." He gestured to one of the other officers.

Juan approached her on Hackney's other side. "Carol, you need to listen to what she has to say."

"Ma'am, this police officer has been aiding this rogue agent," Hackney insisted. "Officers, take him into confinement too."

The Deputy Director stated, "That's absurd. He's my brother-in-law. What's going on here, Juan?"

"It's best we talk privately, Carol."

Hackney leaned in toward the Deputy Director. "Ma'am, it's advised that you don't do this. These two are very dangerous, and we must interrogate them to get to the truth."

I blurted out, "The truth is, you kidnapped my friend and were about to do the same to me!" I said. "Ma'am, I'm sorry to be so direct, but you'd better be on the side of the good guys if you want to hear what I have to say."

Before she could answer, Hackney's voice bellowed, "Gun! Gun! Gun!"

I hurled myself to the floor as two shots erupted. Hackney hit the ground, his weapon still firmly in his grasp. Juan steadied his own gun, pointing it directly at Hackney.

Security grabbed the Deputy Director and were about to lead her away when she shouted, "Stop!"

Juan was forced flat to the ground, hands bound behind him.

"Carol, he's one of the bad guys and just tried to take down the only FBI agent who knows what's really going on!" Juan yelled out.

"Put me down this instant!" The Deputy Director stepped toward me, then glanced at all the guns pointed in our direction. "Put away those guns before anyone else gets hurt . . . *now!*"

They all complied.

"Ambulance is on the way!" an agent called out from across the room.

Another agent kneeling by Hackney said, "He has no pulse."

She looked around the room as though she was trying to put pieces together in her head, then looked down at Hackney again. "Search both of them for other weapons, and then I want to talk to them in a private room. Mrs. Dark, might we use an office space?"

Trevor was visibly anxious, looking at Sarah, who appeared unfazed.

"You can use my office," she said. "It's down the hallway. I'll walk you there."

Sarah leading the Deputy Director away wasn't a good development.

"Deputy Director, wait!" I yelled as someone searched my body for weapons. Then they grabbed both of my arms and pushed me, along with Juan, through the mob after her.

The security agent escorting Juan knocked on a door.

"Just a moment!"

I murmured to Juan, "I don't like this."

He didn't reply. He remained calm and collective, as though he knew everything would work out all right. He glanced at me and winked. I didn't have the same perspective.

I stayed still so their grip on me would loosen some, but they kept their hold firm. I wasn't sure how I could fight them with one injured arm, but I'd do my best.

The door opened, and the Deputy Director said, "Come in, Juan. I'm sorry about this, but I'm still trying to understand what happened here. Please have a seat."

The officers helped us into chairs.

"Gentlemen, we don't need to be so firm," the Deputy Director said.

The agents stepped back against the wall and crossed their arms.

"Carol, it appears that agents from the FBI have been involved in some unsavory activities on an international scale with Dark Enterprises. Agent Jenna Slade has managed to uncover more evidence than anyone had anticipated despite multiple attempts on her life. Agent Kimmel was involved as well."

"Yes, I heard about Kimmel. We weren't particularly close, but I knew her fairly well. Mrs. Hanvey-Dark informed me she suspected there was a criminal organization within her company and has been trying to investigate it without making any announcements. Agent Slade just put the puzzle pieces together faster than anyone expected."

"Ma'am, I'm certain we've found all the evidence necessary to prove who is behind this corruption," I said calmly. "I have personally seen proof that Dark Enterprises, Scelisi, other agents, as well as wealthy people and leaders all around the world are involved. I have documentation of bank accounts and trust funds and the correlation of benign construction supplies masking the shipment of weapons."

The Deputy Director sighed heavily, a hint of turmoil in her expression. "Yes, the evidence sounds substantial. But the real challenge lies with you, Sarah, in finding out who within your organization was responsible."

Sarah nodded. "We won't rest until every person involved is brought to justice."

I clenched my fists, fury bubbling up inside me. "It's not just about the evidence, ma'am—they killed a woman in my home and even tried to take my life! Justice must be served!"

"Where is the evidence, Agent Slade?" the Deputy Director asked—or, more like demanded.

"It's all with Agent Scelisi, who appears to be the only remaining corrupt agent involved in this crime," Juan said. "You can find him tied up at the apartment above Ming's Diner. In downtown Calle Ocho."

I looked at Juan in shock and confusion. The only one remaining? Then it hit me. Kimmel said she was working for a senior FBI leader who was a "she."

The Deputy Director had a sinister look in her eyes, as though she knew more than she was willing to let on. My heart raced as I realized what they were asking me to do. The Deputy Director was supporting Dark Enterprises and Sarah Hanvey-Dark. Was Sarah really going to get away with this?

"Agent Fuller," the Deputy Director said to one of the agents standing against the wall. "Will you send a detail there and gather Scelisi and the evidence? I want all of it accounted for and sent to my office. And Fuller, I need you to oversee this personally—no mistakes."

"Yes, ma'am."

He and the agent next to him walked out the door, leaving just the two agents who had escorted Juan into the room.

"Agent Slade, I express my sincere gratitude for your bravery and determination. You are an exemplary agent who deserves a promotion. I do not doubt that great things await you."

Hanvey-Dark's words made me look to Juan, who gave a slow nod. I felt indignant, though I knew better than to show or voice it.

"Juan, how about joining me for dinner tonight? It's been a long time since Donna's funeral, and I apologize for not checking up on you since then," the Deputy Director said.

"I would love to, Carol."

"Agent Slade, you are free to go. And please send any damages you incurred to me personally. I'll see to it that you are compensated for your losses. Juan, can you follow through with the police to ensure she's no longer Miami's most wanted?"

"I'll take care of it."

My mind raced back and forth between relief and guilt.

"Wait, I . . . what about Kenny?"

The air felt still as everyone looked at each other in confusion.

The Deputy Director asked, "Who's Kenny?"

"He's an elderly neighbor who Hackney abducted the other day. I'm afraid that he's in a cell somewhere."

She pursed her lips and shook her head. "I'll find him, but get some rest, Jenna," she said. "I'll be in touch with you shortly."

I nodded silently, worried that they wouldn't find Kenny alive, and guilty for not doing more to save him myself. Part of me felt like I had failed horrifically.

"Thank you, Deputy Director."

"I'll drive you home," Juan said as he followed me out the door. "Carol, I have the same number. Just call me when you're available."

"I'll do that, Juan, and thank you."

Back in the car, I turned to Juan.

"Why do I feel like we just failed?"

"The Deputy Director is in a delicate position right now, and she'll do the right thing. Unfortunately, it may not be the right thing we'd expect."

"But all those high-level people in the middle of this? What happened to 'No one is above the law?' "

"Sadly, that's not altogether true," Juan said. "I think some people will be punished. You did a good thing, Jenna. Your father would be proud of you."

We drove in silence as I stared out the window, wondering if all I did was even worth the effort, given all those who had died.

Chapter 33

A crowd of FBI agents and cadets assembled in the hall of the FBI Academy in Quantico, Virginia, as the Director addressed them from behind a podium. The Deputy Director stood in front of a chair behind him. She smiled at me, reassuring me what I did was right.

I stood in the back of the auditorium, in front of the doors waiting to walk down the grand aisle. This time it wasn't to receive my badge, it was to receive an award. An award I wasn't sure I earned, or at least wasn't sure the guilty were disciplined. It's been two weeks since that day I met with the Deputy Director, and two weeks of soul-searching on what happened, what Juan influenced to happen, what likely would always happen when the powerful are consumed by greed.

"We are expected to uphold a high standard when dealing with criminals, no matter how tempting it may be to accept luxuries that our wage can't provide. It's the honor we hold to ensure the safety of a nation, which is the greatest reward we can ask for. Agent Jenna

Slade is a perfect example. Her courage and moral conviction were necessary to keep us safe from the dangers we face."

The Director's eyes landed on me. "Agent Slade, will you come up here?"

My gaze went to Kenny, who stood beside me near the back of the hall. He nodded and gave a slight wink. "You got this. And Jenna?"

"Yeah?"

"I've got your back."

Walking down the aisle, I scarcely heard the thunderous clapping. I thought about those who died, Kimmel, my uncle, Jefferies, Wilson, Porter, and even Baxter, and the corrupt elites who would likely get away with all their crimes. But one thing I was able to accomplish was exonerating my father and placing his name on the wall of honorable deaths within the Bureau. The Deputy Director had made the change for my father, provided the replacement funds for the destruction in my home, and put Scelisi away into a maximum-security prison for a very long time. The public announcement named him as the leader of the entire smuggling ring.

Although I vowed to never be bought, I realized what it took to stay alive. Everything I did here probably only set the operation back a few months—maybe a year. They would restart it, and the same people would be in place to get it going again. I looked up to strong female leaders but realized they were no better than the men, possessing same lack of morals and integrity.

"Agent Slade, we have awarded you the FBI Medal of Valor for demonstrating the courage, loyalty, and conviction that our noble institution was founded upon. You are truly an inspiration for all of us to remind ourselves when we are performing our nation's duty. Congratulations."

The entire auditorium erupted into applause.

The Deputy Director had let Scelisi take the fall. But my gut told me Sarah Hanvey-Dark was the true ring leader.

"Thank you, Director," I said as he placed the medal around my neck.

"I have a new organization," he said. "I'm standing up to fight the very crimes you've uncovered. I could use someone that our country can trust. I hope you'll consider it. Do you have any words to say?"

I thought about all that I went through, the deceit, the killings, the setups, and Kimmel, and wanted to tell everyone everything. I wanted to highlight that the corruption went all the way up to the vice president of the United States.

"No, sir. Thank you, and I'm proud to serve my country."

"Let's have another round of applause for Senior Agent Jenna Slade. An inspiration to the FBI and our country!" he said, and everyone clapped again.

I turned and stepped toward the Deputy Director and shook my hand, she pulled me in close and whispered, "Sometimes the end results are not what we hope they will be, but believe me, Jenna, you made a significant impact."

Juan was in the back of the room, clapping and nodding. He pointed up, and then to me. I knew he was telling me my father was watching. I nodded back, fighting the tears forming in my eyes.

Chapter 34

Apparently, Kenny had a brother in DC who he wanted to visit, so I flew back to Miami with Juan. I wanted to know more about my father when he was younger, and Juan told me many stories. It was the first time I'd laughed in a long time. He told me of some pranks they pulled while at the police academy, and some of the crazy things they did as partners while on the Miami police force.

We rounded the corner into my neighborhood when I asked, "Do you think my father is alive?"

He thought about it for a moment, nodding, and then shaking his head. "If anyone could pull it off, it was him. He was one of the most creative SOBs I'd ever known. With that said, I saw the autopsy report, too, and . . ." he paused. "He'd have to be Houdini to have pulled that off."

I'd have to agree, but so much happened that someone had to have guided me, and from what I found out about Scelisi, I could line him out.

As we pulled into my driveway, I leaned over and put my arms around Juan. "Thank you so very much. I couldn't have done this without you."

"I just helped a little at the end. You did all the work. Oh, by the way. I have a little present for you."

He reached behind the passenger seat and gave me a large manila envelope.

"What's this?"

"Just open it," he encouraged.

I opened the flap and pulled out all the documents that were on the hard drive.

"Where did you get this? I thought it was all turned in." I riffled through the many pages.

"When you connected that drive to my laptop, I saved it to a folder instead of closing it out."

"What should I do with it?"

"Well, that's a good question. You can just let things go right now, or cause a wrinkle in the system. Right now, though, I think you have a visitor."

I slid the documents back into the envelope and looked out the window—Hamilton?

When I looked at Juan in surprise, he just nodded. I grabbed my duffel bag from the back seat and ran to the house.

"Hey, Jenna!"

"Hamilton! I . . . I thought you were dead."

"I was, or am . . . kind of."

We sat outside on the porch as he told me the story of how an older man had found him and explained the risk he and I were in. "He devised a scheme to fake my death, to keep the bad guys off me after I sent you the information."

"That's fabulous. Who was this guy?"

"I don't know. He never gave me a name, but after I saw the material I sent, I realized I needed to trust someone."

"Well, it sounds like you had a guardian angel watching over you. I can't tell you how many times I felt the same way. Now, let's go see what's left after the government hired contractors to clean everything up while I was gone."

We walked inside to see a house that had still clearly been through some things—furniture was missing. Still, the floors were clean again, and the refrigerator was closed but empty. The freezer contained absolutely no ice cream.

As we headed for my father's office, Hamilton said, "It seems you might be ready to put it on the market?"

"Yeah, the thought briefly crossed my mind."

In the office, the blood stain from Porter was gone, and the windows had been replaced.

Hamilton walked to the back, where there was a built-in bookshelf.

"They left some pictures," he said.

"Great, at least I have that."

"Hey, this is the guy!"

"What guy?" I walked up to him.

"The guy who helped me fake my death."

Stunned, I took the picture from him, stared at it, and then looked at Hamilton. "Are you sure?"

"Yeah, why. Who is he?"

"He's my father."

"Shut up! No way."

"And he's supposed to be dead."

"Whoa. Well, regardless, I hope to meet him again to say thanks."

"How did you get here, Hamilton?"

"He got me on a private plane to Baltimore, then on another flight down here. It's a lot more challenging to find a flight for cash, but I guess your father gave me a lot to make it happen, and told me who to contact and where to meet you."

I wiped away the tears on my cheek. I couldn't fault my father for leaving, but he owed me to see him again. "Hamilton?"

"Yeah?"

"Let's go on a vacation. I happen to know just the place."

"I'd love to, but I need to become alive again."

I laughed. "I think I can make that happen. I mean, I did get the Medal of Valor, after all."

"Great. Where are we going?"

"How would you like to take a trip to Switzerland? I hear it's beautiful this time of year, and I have a gorgeous dress I'd like to wear out. I think you'll like it."

I went to my room and placed the documents Juan gave me in my hiding spot, and contemplated what to do next. I was no longer a loose end. They—whoever they are—ensured that I received the credit for uncovering a massive corruption effort that spanned the globe, but all evidence was taken, and one corrupt FBI agent took the fall. Hell, even Dark Enterprises was still investigating who within their company had been involved. Doubt that would come to fruition.

Now that I knew how the game was played, I would likely continue to investigate and take them all down, but it would take time.